Juice

A J Shaw

Grosvenor House
Publishing Limited

This book is published by
Grosvenor House Publishing Ltd
Link House
140 The Broadway, Tolworth, Surrey, KT6 7HT.
www.grosvenorhousepublishing.co.uk

This is a work of fiction. Names, characters, businesses, places,
events, locales, and incidents are either the products of the author's
imagination or used in a fictitious manner. Any resemblance to actual
persons, living or dead, or actual events is purely coincidental.

A CIP record for this book
is available from the British Library

ISBN 978-1-83975-472-2

Dedication

To Eanna, Leah and Oli, may you shine on you crazy diamonds. To Colin, may you always be the emperor of your own universe. To the reader, may you make bad life choices and revel in the moment.

Chapter 1: A childish idea

Sun flickered through the half-closed swaying blinds. James stubbed his third Marlboro Gold of the morning out in an overflowing ashtray that sat on a worn-out coffee table. He had only moved into the small 1 bed in Clapham a month before. Everything seemed so slow now. Yesterday's paper was spread across the rest of the table filling any voids of empty space. Stained half empty cups of tea filled in the blanks. A television mumbled quietly to itself in the corner of the room and a clock kept the rhythm of the morning up on the wall, it was 10.53 and time seemed to sit still in the tight little flat.

Outside the sounds of the bustle of London life could be heard, the hissing of a bus at the nearby stop, the idling of engines purring, a distant siren scurrying to any number of emergencies and uber drivers shouting down their phones on loudspeaker discussing far away homes and inconvenient traffic. James sat back on the shabby sofa and allowed these small details to sink in, he may not of had a job, but he was certainly no slob. He sat in a pair of smart grey tailored trousers, sky blue socks and a pale blue shirt with the sleeves rolled up. Sat next to him was the evidence on his laptop of an ongoing job search.

He had left the Royal Military Academy Sandhurst with an ongoing knee injury; the wound was still fresh; not so much on the body but in the mind. He would lay awake imagining what could have been, the man he could have become, he still spoke to people out of his platoon. They would be walking up the stairs of Old College soon, swords in hand ready to join their regiments on an adventurous journey into the unknown. He had left with a suitcase and several boxes crammed into a Peugeot 208 GTI, nothing more than a handshake and 3 months wages to see him off into the world.

James didn't like the idea of a mundane civilian life, he never had and probably never would. Right now, he needed the money so he scoured the internet applying for every bleak and grey job that would allow ends to meet. That being said he had been careful to save as much as he could before getting out of the army and the 3 months' pay, they gave him made for a good buffer. He pulled his fourth cigarette from its packet and ran it through his fingers before lighting it with an art deco style silver cigar lighter. The smoke burst and danced around the choking room.

With no rush to be anywhere and little motivation for a sedated existence he daydreamed for a while longer, playing out schemes in his head. Perhaps a big win at the roulette table or some far flung adventure would present itself, he could steal some diamond for a thrill, stick up the local dealers for a rush or become some kind of vigilante who beat evil bitter men to a pulp just to feel alive. The pit of his stomach felt uneasy as he looked back to the jobs page. Some office management role at some bland company with a washy bullshit opening speech about hiring people who wanted to achieve the best of their ability. History doesn't remember those who take the easy option or those who sit idly doing an average job whilst they wait for the end credits when they get bowel cancer at 53.

Something caught his eye mid thought, BBC news was playing in the background, a bustle of blue lights flickered in the background and the world-famous police tape violently yanked in the wind behind a straight-faced reporter who expelled some exciting solemn news. Across the bottom of the screen floated the words 'Breaking News: Daring robbery in Chiswick three men have been arrested, police seek fourth'. And with that the screen flicked back to the studio, James had missed the story, but it would be on the website and all over the papers for sure, he opened a new tab and searched the BBC news.

As he read the story his eyes lit up with glee and a small smile crept across his face. Last night around 11.42pm a four-man gang had broken into Metropolitan Safe Deposits on Chiswick High Rd. A JCB digger was used to smash through the front of the building and then 'precision equipment' was used to access the individual boxes inside. None of the members who had been caught were in possession of any of the stolen goods, several firearms were recovered when ARV officers from CO19 (London's elite firearms unit) had chased them down. Each member of the gang had left on separate stolen scooters, mostly vespas with no number plates and one had been clipped in the arm when he hadn't listened to instructions and decided to close down one of the responding officers. He was in a stable condition apparently. The value of the stolen boxes was yet to be established but experts believed this was a targeted raid that could easily be in the millions. It was also unknown what was actually stolen as the company held no records of the what was kept inside the individual boxes.

The fourth suspect was still at large and was seen fleeing the scene on a T-max scooter with a black grip bag slung over his shoulder. It was believed that he may have switched vehicles later down the line and it was still unknown if anyone else was involved. James imagined being at the scene as everything had happened, the excitement must have been unreal on both sides. It was rare to see this kind of organised robbery anymore, never mind someone actually getting away with it. No doubt as he sat on the shabby sofa, officers from Scotland Yard would be combing through every scrap of CCTV and detectives on the scene would be gathering every slither of evidence with meticulous precision. It probably wouldn't take long to catch the guy, it never really did anymore.

James decided that sooner or later he needed to go outside and so he stopped off at a local café to pick up some lunch before wondering down to Battersea Park. His phone never rang anymore, his friends resided around the same pubs or sat quietly in their hovels around London immersing themselves in online games and growing stale smoking weed alone in dark rooms. After becoming far too vocal about his disdain for such a life he had been cut off and left to drift away, he often felt like he had broken free from an anchor and now floated towards the surface of an ever-expansive sea. For now, though it was a lonely race to the surface and into the unknown.

As he gently strolled through pedestrians and the noise of busy streets towards the oasis of the park James couldn't get the robbery out of his head. Again, and again the scene played out as if he was sat on the side of the road whilst a JCB smashed through plate glass and brickwork. He could hear the thieves shouting commands to each other as they relayed information and got to work on the boxes, perhaps they blew the locks off or maybe they froze them and then smashed them off with sledgehammers. He could picture the lookout breathing heavily through his ski mask and brandishing some kind of shotgun. The shotgun bit was mostly his imagination running wild, but he liked the idea of it.

James took a bite from his sandwich as he watched the world pass him by. The sun flickered through the leaves and the trees swayed in the gentle breeze like drunks waiting for the last bus home. He had an idea, a foolish and farfetched idea that crept into his mind as he sat isolated on his worn-out tranquil bench. What if he found the bag? Somewhere in London right now a thief sat with a black grip bag with potentially millions of pounds, it could be diamonds or cash who could know? He flirted with the idea, toying with it in his mind as he nibbled away at his second-rate café lunch. He didn't even like the food but the girl behind the till was cute, not that he would ever actually talk to her. He bounced ideas through his head of how he could possibly find out who the thieves were. Maybe if he looked up stolen scooters, or he could find out who owned the boxes that were stolen. There was every chance they had enemies; if you had the wealth and cunning to require a safe deposit box you were sure to have people around you that were more than willing to watch you fall to your knees. One thing was for sure, if he sat tight for long enough more information would trickle out from the media over the next few days. James smiled to himself and sighed, of course he would never actually see it through, it was little more than a child's excitement running rampant in his own head. His piercing blue eyes looked up in contemplation and he raised his dark brown eyebrows, an idea. A plausible idea as well. He needed to find Charlotte, she always had her ear to the ground, a good cocktail bar and some gossip would surely coax her out of her shell.

Chapter 2: The Rave

The dull sound of repetitive thuds carried over a dilapidated corner of Willesden, it echoed through the winding canals and backstreets. It bounced off the walls of warehouses and industrial playgrounds. Through the black night, illuminated by the orange glow of the streetlamps, revellers pilgrimaged towards the distinctive sound. Only visible in small groups or maybe the odd car speeding off in the direction of the racket, the closer you got the louder it became and the more distinct the sounds.

As the random trickle of people turned around a final corner they were faced with an industrial estate and a warehouse. A loading bay door was cracked ajar and a fire exit chained back being manned by a menacing, looming man in a black hooded jacket and a conveniently heavy flashlight. With every step the thumping became louder, more volatile and noticeably more rhythmic. Outside; groups of the strange and quirky, the disobedient or those who knew no different queued eagerly to enter, some with piercing eyes and black holes for pupils. Most with a bounce in their step, a few who pouted with hoods up and hands in pockets, eager for trouble.

Once inside two separate sound systems raged, one playing aggressive volatile tekno that made your heart hit your ribs with every beat, the other was situated in a separate part of the warehouse in what would have been the offices and played jump up drum and bass. The mood was electric, thousands moved to the rhythm with so much energy that through the lasers and strobe lights it looked like a giant pan was bubbling over. Everywhere the stench of skunk and hash wafted through the crowd and young entrepreneur drug dealers and runners called out their stock to passing ravers, 'MD, Coke, Pills...'. The drugs ran free and the sound systems shook the very core of the building and vibrated through the walls.

Various shades of freak could be found in the space, hood rats and roadmen, new age hippies, anarchists, university students and local kids looking for an adventure but within this mix lay a far more dangerous animal. Parties such as this attracted big money, and with-it big criminals, some of them predators with big smiles whilst others violent and sporadic. With the right eyes you could spot them in the crowd, still and calm whilst surrounded by the chaos, cold eyes and stern faces poking out through the ecstasy of the moment, only concerned with money and reputation. The rave scene for them was nothing but a means to an end and a method of moving drugs and hiding other illicit dealings.

In a back room away from the dancing and partying a young man no older than 17 sat on a grubby old wooden chair, his arms were tied to the arm rests and his legs were tied to the feet. His breathing was heavy and a bead of sweat trickled from his temple, his deep brown eyes showed nothing but fear. He broke down slightly and begged to be let go, but his pleas fell on deaf ears. Outside the locked door the rumble of the deep bass was ever persistent. He wore an adidas tracksuit and his Nike satchel lay strewn a few feet away, his fingers trembled consistently and every now and again he would swallow deeply, needless to say he knew he was very much fucked.

Colin stood in front of him, a slender, lanky man about 5'11 around 50 years old with slicked back dark brown hair that fell past his ears. He wore heavy black combat boots with worn-in dark grey jeans, a black t-shirt and a dusty black bomber jacket. He was rolling a cigarette and his dark piercing eyes stared at his handy work through his silver framed glasses. His face was wrinkled and hard with a layer of dirt that made the character pop out. He spoke in a harsh Manchurian accent, 'Listen kid I just don't get it, all we want to know is what you were bragging about to your little mates down on the dance floor', he smiled menacingly. 'I don't want to see you hurt over nothing, I mean Simon might, but I've never enjoyed all this violence'.

Simon stood a meter or two behind the chair in the shadows, the personification of violence. He was also in his 50's, short and stocky. He had short neat grey hair with a rat tail that protruded below his collar, his hands showed years of fighting with broken flat knuckles and down his rough face on the left cheek ran a deep and obvious scar from a knife fight in his youth. His forearms were littered with Celtic style prison tattoos, he wore a tattered red Suzuki t-shirt, green combat trousers and steel toecap boots. He smiled to himself calmly at Colin's words as he toyed with a drill that he was brandishing. In his free hand he held a dozen or so extra-long masonry screws.

The kid stuttered and struggled to no avail, the panic set in and he thrashed wildly, when all else failed he screamed 'HELP!'. No one came, no one could hear him, the outside world was in ignorant bliss. Simon took a few steps forward and with total calmness and clarity lined the first screw up with the boy's forearm and quickly and neatly drilled it into the tattered wooden chair. The material of his tracksuit twisted and wrapped with the screw as it burrowed its way in, and a small spurt of crimson blood shot up as it found home. He screamed a blood curdling scream, true agony and terror.

'Now please kid, I'll ask again, from what I understand you were smoking a joint downstairs and well you were bragging to your friends about selling some stolen scooters for a robbery'. He paused momentarily. 'The thing is, we would really like to know more, so please in your own time... tell us the story'. Colin had squatted next to the kid and put his hand on his shoulder as if to comfort him. He put the freshly rolled cigarette in the kids' mouth, lit it, then paused looking him dead in the eye before standing up and immediately rolling another. Simon meanwhile was lining up the next screw ready to put his handy skills to good use.

'Bruv I'm begging you I don't even know that much', the distinct sound of the drill kicked in again followed almost immediately by the same horrific scream, this one bled far more profusely and immediately began dribbling blood onto the floor. 'Woooo, listen you little cunt I don't actually care if you talk, I'm having fun just like this', Simon whispered as he grinned from over the kids shoulder before walking to a table in the corner putting the drill down and snorting an alarmingly long line of cocaine that was racked waiting for him.

'Ok ok ok ok... I swear fam I lifted a bunch of peds from Central and we were selling them and that, so some brare hits me up on the insta page we were selling them through saying he wants to buy like fucking six of them or some shit, we thought they were feds or something, they seemed well sketch but they were offering P, I mean proper P for them, so we took the risk, anyway two days later we meet these guys in Peckham Rye where we'd been stashing all the shit, two guys show up, they were tooled up and they looked like they meant fucking business, proper G shit you know.. so, we sell them the peds, they fucking stick them all in this van, and leave, we get like 3 grand for it. Basically, one of the olders from the estate happened to be rolling through and tells us after that those guys are proper badmen and he saw one of them hanging out in Dam doing shady shit with diamonds back in the day when we were still proper kids. They came from Essex or some shit'. The kid spat his words out rambling through the pain and with as much detail as he could bare to remember. The bike thief had come out to celebrate a big win and ended up tied to a chair.

Colin cackled with a wide smile and clapped slowly, 'One second', he walked over to the table where Simon had racked him up an equally terrifying line which he snorted, twitched and walked back to centre stage. 'You see that wasn't hard, now we can be friends, like I said there's no need for any of this violence, how about we get you untied and on your way… ooo, actually one last thing, we need to know exactly what these guys looked like', Colin had squatted back down to the kids eye level put his hand under his chin and lifted the thief's head to make eye contact one last time. The hideous whirring of the drill came back into play over the sound of the rave outside.

Chapter 3: Meeting at Bar Américain

James walked up the steps of Piccadilly Circus tube station with a bounce in his step, it was already dark outside, and the lights and adverts of the famous landmark dazzled and illuminated the scores of tourists who stood around marvelling at London's magnetic beauty. James always dressed for the occasion, wearing a brown tweed sports jacket, a green moleskin waistcoat with a gold pocket watch with a fox fob, his favourite tailored trousers and a pair of black brogues. His tie was royal blue with a gold stripe and for a pocket square he wore gold and red Japanese silk. Everything about the outfit said subtle class and style, very few dressed like this anymore. He always felt you should make a statement with an outfit and besides he was meeting Charlotte and god knew she would be wearing something exquisite and classic. She loved to turn heads.

He saw a break in the traffic and skipped and jogged across the road towards Brasserie Zédel which was just around the corner sitting on the very edge of Soho. The door man greeted him and opened the heavy art deco door and invited James in. The place was a hidden gem, if you knew then you knew, he slid through the café and down some stairs at the back which were littered with old 1920's film and jazz posters and into a stunning courtyard that split between three rooms. The restaurant, the concert room and Bar Américain. The décor and setting were truly amazing, and one could easily become lost in the fantasy of living in a bygone era if you stayed down there for long enough. The building had once been a classy art deco hotel and it had maintained its class and charm into its new life with grace.

A waiter invited James into the bar, showed him to a dimly lit table and left him with the menu. Jazz noir played softly in the background and the low lighting left moody shadows cutting through the room and the harsh angles of the décor. Well-dressed waiters and waitresses scurried politely around with silver trays balancing exquisite drinks, whilst bartenders worked with lighting speed like mad scientists preparing complex and intriguing creations for patrons who discussed politics and fashion, swapped amusing anecdotes and dropped important names into conversation to advance social standings.

Charlotte would be late, she always was, how could she possibly make an entrance if there was no one present to witness it. James ordered an espresso martini and waited patiently whilst enjoying the music in the background, he kept his eyes on the entrance at the far end of the room. A few minutes later the waiter arrived back with his drink. Subtle yet artistic, it was the small details that made it, the way the coffee beans had been placed and the way the hues of brown faded through the stylish glass meeting at the stem. James looked to his watch, he thought she would probably arrive soon. He had taken off the jacket and rolled up the sleeves of his crisp white shirt making for an equally smart but more comfortable look.

They had agreed to meet at 9pm, it was almost 10 past to the second when Charlotte turned the corner to be met by the waiter. Around him it seemed as if the conversations in the room took a momentary pause and just for a second you could hear a pin drop.

Charlotte wore a flowing sky-blue low-cut designer dress that cut off at the knees, white heels and a matching white clutch. Her hair was mousey with a loose wave at the front, the main body was pinned up with a hair slide at the back which glistened in the light with the occasional wink of a diamond. Her makeup was subtle and complemented her soft pretty face but what really stood out to the room was the necklace around her neck. A piece by Van Cleef and Arpels that framed her outfit and beauty in a dazzle of bright white diamonds that left those who gazed upon them blinded.

'James!', she bounced over with a spring in her step and threw her arms out for a hug, James stood up, hugged his old friend and kissed her on the cheek. 'You look fantastic as always', he smiled as he looked her up and down. 'Isn't it just beautiful?' she gestured to the weighty necklace, 'It's truly stunning', James commented with a smile, taking a moment to truly appreciate the craftsmanship up close. It blew his mind that something so small could be worth so much, you could buy the rarest of super cars for the same money. He got lost in his own thoughts for a brief second thinking about all the ridiculous things that you could buy for the price of that gorgeous trinket.

The waiter pulled out a chair to allow Charlotte to sit and they both took their positions on opposite sides of the table. The small lamp in the middle cast a moody shadow across both of their faces as they sat. Charlotte gestured to the waiter before he had a chance to walk away, she didn't need the menu, 'I will have a paloma please', in fact she knew it wasn't on the menu and that was just how she liked it. The waiter nodded politely and swung round to the bar to deliver the instructions to the bartenders. They set to work with little hesitation, you could always judge a good barman not by what was on the menu but how well they adapted to what wasn't on it, and in this place, they never skipped a beat.

'So, James, how is life outside the army, have you gone totally insane yet'? Charlotte inquired, 'A little' he replied. 'I've been looking for work here and there but to be honest I couldn't live with myself if I took half of the jobs on offer', he took a sip from his drink. 'Well I've been living off the properties in Richmond recently, rents are high, and life is good', She smiled gleefully. The waiter arrived with her drink, she thanked him and took a generous sip before placing it down delicately. 'I'm also looking to buy land outside London at the moment, something that can be built on but I'm taking it slow and cautiously, they always try to play a girl like me', she chuckled to herself. James knew all too well that it was normally her who played them. Charlotte had inherited property from her mother and ever since had been working to build a rental empire that wasn't to be sniffed at.

They sat for a while discussing old friends and reminiscing on wild parties and past lovers. Swapping stories from their vastly different existences and Charlotte downloading surreal and bizarre gossip from the rich and obscene around London, tales of affairs and money lost in bad decisions. Her old school friends were all busy making their fortunes or squandering their parents extensive bank accounts travelling around in private yachts and exploring the far-flung corners of the globe in eye watering high class, you couldn't make it up.

'So, I was wondering if you could help me? You always have an ear to the ground with what's going on in London', James said as he finished the last of his drink. 'Of course, James, I'm always happy to help, anything for an old friend', she crossed her legs, intrigued by what could be coming. 'Well you're obviously aware of this recent robbery in Chiswick, the safe deposit boxes and the thief that got away... well do you know anything about it? Whispers from the classy town people'? James presented the question.

'Well it just so happens that I was having lunch with Joanna yesterday and she mentioned something, it's not a lot but it certainly seemed intriguing... what's this all about anyway? You're not planning on becoming a bank robber or something are you? She laughed. 'Not exactly', James replied leaning forward. 'Well I suppose out of pure boredom I wanted to see what I could find out about the whole mess, a bit of amateur detective work if you will, something to pass the time', he waved down the waiter to order a second drink.

'I see, you never could just have a plain life could you, well how exciting, this is what I heard... So Joanna was saying she had dinner with a guy who went to our school called Dimitri, now Dimitri was Russian and got sent over here to boarding school by his father', Charlotte slid back in her chair as she crafter her story, 'no one was sure what his dad did but it was something in the oil industry. There were rumours he had some pretty heavy mafia connections too, so Dimitri was saying that when those boxes got stolen the Russian mafia had gone crazy over it apparently. They're turning over every stone looking for this fourth man who got away. God knows what they stole but it's clearly worth a lot to someone. Now the last thing Joanna mentioned of the whole ordeal was something to do with the gang having connections in Amsterdam's diamond trade and drugs, its farfetched but rumour has it that the thief would have run to Amsterdam the first chance he got'.

Of course, it was all speculation and rumour, James was aware of this, but it was the first nugget of a clue, the first breadcrumb that could lead his wild goose chase in any sense of direction. 'Now that is truly fascinating', he commented. 'I imagine the Russian mafia aren't the kind of people that you want to piss off'. 'Exactly', said Charlotte 'So I expect you to be sensible and don't go doing anything stupid James, we may not see each other much but I do in fact like your company', she gave him a stern look like a parent handing out a warning with little more than their eyes.

The pair spent the rest of the evening sipping on expensive cocktails and spinning tales from the comfort of their chairs until it was time for the night to wind down. Charlotte called her driver to come and collect her, Soho was no place to walk around with a set of jewellery that cost more than the average house. They got the bill, promised not to leave it so long next time and embraced as they stood up. James walked Charlotte back up through the café to the entrance where a very swish black Mercedes waited, a polite man in a black suit opened the rear door and she spun herself in with grace like a dancer, everything was a performance.

James walked around Soho for a while, he took in the scenes of the late night bustle, drunk party goers making racket in the streets, people queued for food and the local homeless cruised the pavements in search of spare change to get a last can of beer in for the night or something to put in their veins, it depended on their poison. He looked up flights to Amsterdam as he walked and hovered over the buy now button, he would sleep on it, maybe he would go anyway, he had wanted to go back to Amsterdam for a while even if he came to a dead end he could still have a nice little break from this job hunt.

Chapter 4: The Professionals

An old Nokia vibrated on a dark wooden table, a moment passed and then it vibrated again. David looked down at the phone as it squirmed around with every burst of sound. It had no caller id which normally meant one thing, work. He picked the relic up and answered it, 'hello', he said briefly. 'Hi David'? the voice on the other end responded, 'speaking', he replied, always keeping his answers brief until he knew exactly who he was talking to. The conversation went on for around 15 minutes, David sat at the table with the phone wedged between his ear and his shoulder, in front of him an A5 moleskin notebook began to fill up with notes, names, addresses and times. A final thing before the conversation ended, the obligatory mention of payment. £10,000 a week for the duration of the job with a £15,000 bonus at the end when the job was done.

Once the person on the other end had hung up David picked another phone up off the table, a Samsung Galaxy. He spent a moment flicking through his contacts until he found his partner Mike. The phone rang for a few seconds before there was an answer 'Dave', Mike said with a chirpy upbeat voice 'What can I do for you'? 'It looks like we have a job', David replied whilst scratching the side of his head and looking back through the notes he had just written out from the previous conversation, he tapped his pen on the table.

'So, this is what we've got mate, do you remember the deposit box robbery in London the other day? Well our client wants us to find the fourth thief that got away or at the very least get the stuff that was stolen back'. He stretched his neck from side to side and continued. 'So, intel looks like we're looking for a guy called Elliot Wicks, he has previous for assault and did a few years in his early 20's for possession of a firearm. He operated out of Essex, police have already made contact and turned his home life upside down so we'll have to stay away from that, but I have an idea where we can find out where he's going'. David regurgitated the information out of his notebook, meanwhile Mike was most likely sitting at the other end of the phone writing everything down in his own notebook with exact precision.

The evening was drawing in and the wind was picking up throwing some loose rubbish across the quiet suburban street. A black Audi A4 rolled up slowly to David's house and glided to a stop. Before he came out David double checked his pockets, he'd already double checked the windows and locks, it was force of habit. Just before he stepped out of the door he looked over his Walther P99 one last time, took out the magazine and made sure it was fully loaded, there was already one in the breach, he also took the time to ensure the two spare magazines were exactly where he wanted them, he then placed the pistol back in the discreet holster that sat underneath his 5.11 tactical jacket. He was pretty sure he wouldn't be needing firearms tonight, but it was a good insurance policy.

Mike sat in the subtly fast car listening to 'Love is the drug' by Roxy Music, his fingers tapping on the bespoke leather steering wheels to the rhythm, his eyes were always aware of what was going on around him. A dog walker passed by, but he had known before the guy had come around the corner because of the reflection in a car. This kind of hyper awareness took years of practice and experience. Both David and Mike were in their mid-30's wore indistinct outfits and military style short neat haircuts with jeans, boots and black all-weather jackets. The big giveaway was the watches they wore, tactical G-Shocks turned in, so the face was on the inside of the wrist, a sure sign of military experience.

The pair drove up towards Soho and discussed the job at hand, this evening was a fact-finding mission and they knew exactly where to look. If Elliot Wicks wanted to make it out of the country he would have had a contact to arrange new passports and more often than not these things passed through the hands of Charles Abdi, better known as Charlie, a pimp and shady business man that operated out of Soho. The son of a Turkish father an English mother and brought up around Stratford the man had built himself a small empire around the city and an expansive network that spread like a web across the city's streets. Of course, it was safe to say Mr Abdi rarely touched any of the dirty work himself but most likely a single phone call and he could find out who had and when.

As night drew in the lights on the A3 brought an atmosphere to the drive, headlights and flashes of red from breaks up ahead created a light show for drivers trying to just focus on their journeys as they flew down tarmac arteries in and out of the city. 'If we find out everything we need tonight we can get a plane in the morning', Mike pondered as they drove, he kicked the car up a gear and the engine roared for a brief second whilst it whipped its way past some idiot in a Fiat Panda sitting lazily in the middle lane idly unaware of anything around it. 'It sounds like we'll most likely end up in Amsterdam if the intelligence is correct, my one concern is that if Elliot is going to Amsterdam I doubt he's planning on hanging around for very long and we have no idea as of yet where he would plan on going from there', Mike continued milling his thoughts out loud.

David spoke up, 'Once we've spoken to Charlie we can come up with a solid game plan, we can put our usual shopping list to the guys in Europe so we'll have a vehicle and all the toys waiting for us wherever it is we end up flying into. I hope you don't mind I requested the new Audi Q7, I used one on a protection job in Monaco a few months ago and it drove beautifully'. Mike nodded in agreement 'No problem at all mate, I heard good things, I've heard a couple of the boys have been trying them out recently, they're pretty sexy too'. The conversation changed to cars for a while, German cars still seemed to rule supreme but Japanese engineering had a precision edge. Both agreed, fuck buying anything French on principle, obviously this was tongue in cheek, and they chuckled.

After a while the car swung round into the West End. The city was alive, it always was. As they passed through Piccadilly Circus a well-dressed man skipped and jogged through a break in the traffic in front of them. As they crawled deeper into Soho people took their lives in their hands. Tourists dived through ever riskier gaps and Deliveroo riders buzzed like wasps at breakneck speeds in every direction. They parked the car off the street in a 24-hour carpark that may as well have been robbing the punters on the way in with the prices they were charging. Who cares though, they would just claim it all back on the expenses anyway. From the carpark to the office only took a few minutes, they weren't expected, they never were.

Mike rang the buzzer for a flat on the third floor, a few moments passed and so he rang again... 'Who is it?', a woman's voice asked abruptly through the crackled little speaker like it was something out of a cheap 80's sci fi film. 'It's Mike and Dave, we're here to see Charlie, we've got some business', the pair waited for a second. 'Charlie's not here and he hasn't mentioned a Mike or Dave before... maybe ring him', the girl on the speaker replied in the same short tone, her accent sounded foreign, maybe Eastern European. You couldn't really be mad at her; at the end of the day she clearly had a job to do and you could never be too careful in this world. A grey Mercedes 500 was parked in the street, Charles Abdi was definitely in. 'Listen love please just tell Charlie that we're here or next time he wants someone to stalk his wife around town to see who she's fucking we'll start charging'.

The buzzer droned and the latch could be heard unlocking, David pushed the door open and stepped inside. Mike checked their arcs outside before following suit and ensuring the door was closed behind him to prevent any unwanted tailgaters. The pair climbed the narrow staircase, the corridors were dirty and old, a lightbulb flickered desperately clinging on for life, the wallpaper was stripping away, and, in some places, it was gone completely. The whole building smelt damp and unloved. Every so often a piece of banister would be missing. On the second-floor thumping music could be heard from behind the door, the only sign of life in the godforsaken hole of a building. Once they reached the flat on the 3rd floor Charlie opened the door and greeted them like long lost friends with his arms out.

Mr Abdi was a man past his prime, slightly overweight and unshaven. His redeeming features were his expensive clothes and the several gold rings he wore. 'Boys, it's good to see you, come in, come in, come in', he ushered them inside.

Charlie knew very well that he may well be a big shark in this ocean but men like David and Mike were mythical fucking creatures that would quite happily skin a dangerous sea creature alive and wear it as a coat at the first sign that they were in danger of being messed around beyond the point of professionalism. Charlie walked ahead into an office at the end of the narrow hallway. Although it still felt worn and old the inside was a stark contrast to the state of the rest of the building.

Charlie half waddled to a well-stocked drinks cabinet in his office and offered the pair a drink, they both declined but he poured himself a substantial glass of Johnnie Walker Blue Label whisky and dropped backwards into a leather swivel chair with worn out arms and cracks in the leather. Everything about the place felt like a used car dealership or as if once upon a time it had been fairly good quality but had been allowed to gather dust and corrode. Outside the office the girl from the speaker lurked around. She was most likely one of Charlie's more attractive working girls that he would keep back for the right client or a special occasion. Tonight, it would seem she was playing the role of his p/a as she shuffled papers and tinkered away occasionally on a surprisingly fresh-looking computer that sat in the next room over.

'So, gentlemen, to what do I owe the pleasure? I am no fool, I know this isn't a social call-so just fire away and I will see what I can do to help... I hope you appreciate I have always enjoyed our working relationship...' As Mr Abdi was speaking David slipped his black moleskin from his jacket and pulled out a folded-up printout of a man's face. It looked like a mugshot. 'As you're probably aware Charlie, there was a robbery on some safe deposit boxes in Chiswick the other night, we have reason to believe that one of the thieves might have used one of your lads to acquire a new passport before leaving the country, we know a gang from Peckham provided their vehicles'. David slid the photograph across Charlie's desk and leaned back in his chair.

'His name is Elliot Wicks, has previous, works out of Essex and we think he might have connections in Amsterdam but that's yet to be confirmed. What do you reckon Charlie, any ideas'? Whilst David was briefing Charlie, Mike had become very aware of the young escort sat outside of the room, he could feel her listening and when he turned round she tried desperately hard to look busy, shuffling piles of nothing and clicking away at what was probably a blank screen. If the room had a door, he would have closed it. Charlie nodded as he looked at the photograph with intense concentration before breaking his gaze. 'Let me make a phone call gentleman, if he came through my house it will be easy to find out', the plump Turkish man picked up a mobile from his top drawer and fumbled with the screen for a moment. When the person on the other end answered the pair erupted into fast paced Turkish like an auctioneer and a horse race commentator in some weird slam poetry competition.

The conversation went on for several minutes and the name Elliot Wicks was repeated several times. Every time the name was said Charles Abdi would look back to the photograph and nodded to whatever information was being said on the other end. Just before the phone call came to an end Mr Abdi looked around his desk, grabbed a scrap of paper and slammed it in front of him before scrawling some details out. He unceremoniously dropped the pen down before hanging up, the phone was chucked back into the draw with little care and Charlie grabbed his whisky, leant back and took a large sip before placing it back down.

'Ok guys, this is what I've got...' He pushed the scrap of paper across the table back to the pair sitting opposite. 'Elliot Wicks collected a new passport from outside of London just last night from one of my associates, an Australian one apparently, he has a new name of course, John Murphy, I imagine if you use some contacts you will never admit to having you can find out if he's left the country and where he's going to'. Mr Abdi smiled, happy with his work, he shook David and Mike's hands as they left before breathing a sigh of relief once they had gone.

Chapter 5: One-way ticket

Elliot Wicks studied his new passport and repeated the name in his head over and over and over again 'John Murphy, John Murphy'. As the queue moved forward, he shuffled along with it, he slid the passport back into the inside pocket of his jacket and tried to look calm like he was going on a holiday just like everyone else there. It had been an intense couple of days, he thought about the rest of the guys on the job, what had they told the police? Surely his name must be circling every major news channel by now, 'thief at large'. He tried not to think about it too much, he'd barely even escaped the scene of the robbery and even when he did a Fiat Punto almost knocked him off his scooter by pure chance. He still wasn't sure how he had managed to grab the bag before the police descended on the scene.

Victoria Coach Station was as bustling as you would imagine, families with suitcases packed every inconvenient space and the air was filled with chatter and children screaming, a pair of police officers cruised through, Elliot faced his front with his heart in his mouth but no sooner had they appeared they were gone again. He was next in line. 'John Murphy, John Murphy', he repeated in his head again as he pulled the fresh Australian passport back out from his pocket. All he had with him was the black grip bag from the robbery and a rucksack with a wash kit and a spare set of clothes, he had ditched his pistol in a wheelie bin a few hours before, he figured he would pick a new one up when he arrived at the other end fairly easily.

Elliot's eyes looked tired with bags settling below them, he had a five o'clock shadow that was bordering on becoming the start of a beard. He wore a pair of navy blue chinos that could do with an iron and an open neck white shirt with the sleeves rolled up, cheap black shoes and a pair of sunglasses worn on top of the head to keep his short slicked back deep brown hair in position. It was a plain look which allowed Elliot to blend into almost any crowd pretty easily, he looked more like a city banker on his way back from a weekend bender than an armed robber on the run. The young family in front of him finished fumbling with their belongings and bags and trundled off to the side, Dad gathering the passports whilst Mum kept their two young children in check. This was it; Elliot was up.

The woman behind the counter smiled to Elliot and invited him forward 'good afternoon sir, have you already made a booking'? the smile tried to be welcoming but the eyes looked fed up with the constant flow of people. 'No, I haven't actually, would it be possible to book the next coach to Amsterdam please'? his stomach turned but he kept a calm exterior. It was the moments where he had to interact with the public, that he was most likely to draw attention to himself and he'd made it too far to fall before the finish line. The woman clacked away at her computer screen for a few moments, 'that's no problem sir, we have a Megabus leaving in two hours at 13.50', Elliot produced his wallet and new passport, 'that's perfect', he nodded to her with docile satisfaction.

The woman finalised the details and completed the booking, he paid cash, to leave a paper trail with credit cards would be very foolish indeed. The less breadcrumbs Elliot left the police the better, he could feel the paranoia of the detectives closing in, chocking him. He went and bought the most expensive and disappointing sandwich he'd ever seen from a shop around the corner and returned to the coach station to wait quietly in a corner seat. The time went by quickly, he felt hyper aware of everything, he knew the net was closing in on him, but he just didn't know at what point the flying squad would appear out of nowhere. If he made it to Amsterdam then he stood a chance, he needed to keep calm and it would be ok.

It was time, a tired looking ghost of a man in a high-vis jacket stood by the gate and ushered people to start boarding. Elliot prepared his ticket and passport and joined the queue. This was the moment of truth, would his passport work? It looked real but he didn't even have an Aussie accent, the forger had insisted it was the best nationality to pick in the current climate, so Elliot had agreed to trust him. His stomach turned and he felt an irrational sweat set in as he neared the front of the line. When it came time to board, he handed over the paperwork in his hand, the worker in the high vis barely even glanced between the photograph and Elliot Wicks face before handing the documents back and waving him on.

He had done it, the relief took a moment to settle in, but he was through. If he had the same luck at the border he would be laughing. He had to put the grip bag in the storage underneath the coach, this made him feel uneasy, it was the first time he'd let go of the bag in three days but he knew he had no choice and in reality it was probably safer in there than it was in his possession, no one would question it mixed in with all the other bags. Once on the coach he fell asleep almost immediately, he hadn't even realised just how exhausted he was because the next thing he was aware of was the customs border at the Eurotunnel, now this was the real challenge.

Everybody disembarked, stretching and limbering aching limbs that had squeezed into the tight budget seats for several hours as they shuffled out and into the border control office. Panic truly set in this time; did they have his photograph? Would the passport flag up? He swallowed and tried to look as fed up as everyone else, he was desperate not to look around too much or make eye contact with the guards, he needed to act natural but the more he thought about it the less natural he felt like he was acting.

It was time, he handed over the passport, the border guard looked him dead in the eye, Elliot smiled weakly. The guard studied the passport for a short while and flicked through the pages, he returned to the page with the photograph and paused. There was a silent showdown, the tension in the air for Elliot was so intense he wasn't even sure if he had breathed recently. Then the silence was broken he placed the passport back on the counter, 'enjoy your trip Mr Murphy', the guard nodded him through before passing his stern gaze to the next person in the solemn line. Elliot hopped back onto the coach on the other side of the gates and got comfortable back in his seat, he felt genuinely relaxed for the first time. He breathed a subtle sigh of relief and smiled to himself whilst looking out of the window at the scenes of cars lining up waiting to run away on weekend retreats and escapades into Europe.

Elliot imagined what he would do with his new life, the places that he could see, Amsterdam was just the first step, a much needed pitstop to gather supplies and to reset before enacting the next steps of the plan. The rest of the gang may have fallen foul but he had made it and he couldn't sit and worry about the rest of them now. He had himself to worry about and besides they would probably rat him out at the nearest opportunity if it meant a lighter sentence, it's probably what he would do too although he would never admit it. The coach's journey through the Eurotunnel was quiet and peaceful, some people slept, children played quietly and over the relative silence the faint sounds of people's headphones could be heard playing a distant variety of music. Elliot daydreamed of his future life. The bar he would open in some warm and inviting country and the beautiful local wife he was yet to meet; it would be a simple happy life.

Several hours had passed and the coach had arrived in France before pushing north towards Brussels and then into the Netherlands, it was just before Brussels that Elliot's phone rang. This was particularly odd as it was a burner phone he had received from the same man who had provided his passport. No-one had his number, no-one on earth could know whose phone this was. He stared at the screen with fearful wide eyes for what felt like a lifetime, there was no caller id. He didn't want to know who was on the other end, he just wanted to disappear into nowhere and live his daydreams in peace, but the ringing was persistent. He pressed the green button and slowly raised the phone to his ear, '…hello'?

'Good afternoon Elliot Wicks, or I guess we should call you Johnathan Murphy from Sydney now, listen very carefully… you have stolen from some very dangerous and very serious people Mr Wicks, we have been employed to ensure the safe return of what you have in your possession… you have one opportunity and one opportunity alone to stop now and return the stolen goods to our client. If you do not comply, we will find you in due course and you will wish that the police had gotten to you first… return to London immediately and face the music, do you understand'?

Elliot sat in his seat frozen, the only word that stuttered out of his mouth was a whispered 'fuck'. 'We will take that as a yes then Mr Wicks, you have one chance.' The phone went dead. Elliot sat in silence; in a single moment his entire world had come crashing down. He knew that the safe deposit boxes had been targeted and that they had been picked out as the boxes to potentially hold the most value, but he knew nothing of the people he had actually robbed. The voice on the other end of the phone had sounded cold and calm, steely and chilling in a way that pierced his ear and made him want to throw up.

When the bus stopped in Brussels for a moment Elliot stepped off the coach and hesitated before chucking the phone in the bin, at that moment he had made his decision. If he went back to London, he would either end up in custody or very, very dead. Not for a second did he believe that whoever had phoned him would let him live, they were clearly well organised and he was the sort of loose end that they simply wouldn't allow to float off, especially after doing something to draw attention to whoever they were. He wanted to throw up or scream, he did neither but instead walked quietly back onto the coach, he would need to collect his supplies and get out of Amsterdam as quickly as physically possible. The last thing he thought to himself before the coach pulled away towards its final destination was the simple mantra 'trust no one'.

Chapter 6: She could have been a dancer

Lisa sat at the edge of an unmade and messy double bed, she rolled knee high stocking back up her leg and clipped them into her stunning black suspenders that hugged her curved sexual hips. A cigarette hung from her supple lips and she took a deep drag whilst she gathered her belongings and began to sort out the basic and practical hotel room. The client had left, and the money sat on the bed side table. A substantial sum, a small wad of 20- and 50-pound notes, of course Lisa didn't see half of it; it was just the way business was done. She was a songbird in a gilded cage, to be seen and lusted over but never meant to fly free, she hated it to her very core, but she hid it so well. You might even have been fooled into thinking that she enjoyed the company of her various clients. Bankers and lawyers mostly, people with big reputations in the city and even bigger wallets.

She had been working in London for two years, of course this was never the life that she had dreamt of when she left Lithuania, she had always wanted to be a dancer but she soon found out that London was full of false promises. She had lived in a tiny room in Hounslow and had worked in a small local coffee shop that barely paid enough to cover the rent. It was when she was visiting a friend in town that she had met Mr Abdi, originally he told her that he could make her a model, and she certainly was stunning but everything had gone downhill from there and soon enough she found herself under the thumb of Mr Abdi and his associates. She was promised good money to leave Hounslow and move into a room in Soho, all she had to do was entertain the wealthy and she would be looked after. They had made it very difficult to refuse.

A black bob hair cut stopped just before her collar, her skin was pale and fair with classy subtle makeup, her eye shadow made her eyes pop like ocean blue jewels that glistened in the right light. Her slender neck was usually accompanied by a choker style silver necklace with a little silver moon hanging from it, a present from a sister she never got to see. She normally wore stylish short dresses that showed off her hourglass figure, her legs never seemed to end, she was well toned and normally wore short practical heels that complimented her outfit. She knew how to turn heads, but she also knew how to look after herself, her tongue could be as sharp as her nails if you rubbed her the wrong way. She may not have been in control of her own life but that didn't mean she wouldn't give anyone a piece of her mind.

She took another drag from the cigarette and rested her chin on her hand, she looked fed up, Lisa had wanted to escape for so long, but she had nowhere to escape to. She had saved money. She thought of running back home and opening a dance school in her local town, a happy place where all the little girls could do ballet and she could find dignity and peace. Her mind took her back to the previous evening when she had been doing some errands and paperwork for Mr Abdi, the two men had showed up in the office, in all honesty she was glad they had, it meant Mr Abdi would stop trying to feel her up for a while.

The men had talked about a robbery and something worth a lot of money being stolen. Lisa had sat and heard everything. She had pretended to work in the next room so she could listen, she had even taken some notes, where they thought he was going, the name he was using, she had even managed to get a good look at the mugshot the pair had produced and given to Mr Abdi. She had saved a little money but it was nothing really in the grand scheme of things, she had toiled too hard and had little to show for it, she shrugged the idea off, what did she know about hunting down armed robbers with inconspicuous bags? Nothing really. She finished getting dressed, looked herself over in the mirror of the bathroom and left the basic room behind.

Outside it was dark and an uber sat waiting in front of the hotel, she climbed into the back and sat in silence as the taxi weaved its way through the electric back streets of London. Pubs and clubs were alive with people, the lights glowed in stark contrast to the black sky above, the ambience of the London night life felt like the glow of an old film set with every tourist and reveller an actor upon its sprawling stage. The uber didn't take long to reach the familiar streets of Soho and outside the front door of Mr Abdi's sleazy 3rd floor office. Lisa used the key to let herself in and climbed the rickety old staircase up to the office.

She opened the door and walked in, Charlie barely looked up from his desk and grunted a half-hearted hello, the night was slow, and he sat at his desk polishing off a bottle of Bowmore single malt whisky. Mr Abdi normally drank every night, tonight he sat alone and got drunk, he was never pleasant to be around in such a state. Lisa stayed in the next room for a moment, she tried to avoid his company whenever possible, especially when he was in a state like this. She sat on the windowsill and looked down onto the streets below. It made her smile to see happy couples and friends living happy simple lives below blissfully unaware of the creatures that lurked in the shadows of the city.

'Money!', Charles Abdi's voice boomed from the next room, it didn't matter how much he had to drink the man never forgot about money. Lisa and some of the other girls called him Mr Krabs behind his back after the money obsessed crab from SpongeBob SquarePants. They would watch it together with a bottle of red wine when they weren't working and chuckle, doing impressions of Mr Abdi and his greasy sleazy friends that could be found hanging around the office into the small hours during the weekdays. It was little moments of freedom that made the whole thing bearable, quite often the girls would get good cocaine and speed for free and they would party together in a small flat away from the prying eyes of their usual world.

'Money!', Charlie shouted again more aggressively this time, Lisa slid off the window sill and grabbed the little bundle of cash from her purse and stomped through to the other room where Mr Abdi was semi slumped back in his chair, his whisky tumbler sat in front of him on the desk with the bottle to one side, only about a quarter remained. It had been full and unopened when she had left. Lisa placed the money on the table next to the glass, as she placed it down Mr Abdi jolted forward and grabbed her wrist with a violent jerk. 'Why don't you come over here and give me a kiss', he snarled with his alcohol drenched breath, she tried to pull away, but he wasn't having any of it.

'Hey bitch, you'd be nothing without me, you should show a little appreciation', he was stood up now and pulled at her from across the table. Lisa simply tried to turn away, it was normally a bad idea to start an argument, other girls had come to regret it later. She could feel the anger welling up inside of her, sick of being treated like dirt. 'Get off you pig', she blurted out as she pulled away again. This time she broke free and began to walk away but Charlie quickly came around the table. 'You ungrateful fucking whore, I could send you to some shithole brothel down the road if I wanted you slut', he pushed her back against the table and felt her down the thigh.

Lisa was sick of it, she felt degraded and cheap, she thought about the disappointment if her parents could see the position she was in. Mr Abdi forced his tongue into her mouth and then without a thought it happened. She didn't even realise she had done it until it was too late. Lisa pushed Mr Abdi away and picked up the whisky tumbler from off the table and with all her anger and aggression, smashed it in his grotesque drunk face. He gave out a yelp as he tumbled backwards onto the floor holding his face, he knocked paper off shelves and the lamp on his desk came down with him.

The blood poured through his fingers as he writhed around on the floor 'Fuck!... You cunt bitch, I'll kill you!', he rambled various insults whilst curled up and clutching at his face in a helpless pose. Several deep gashes covered his face and a thick shard of glass protruded from his cheek, blood dripped onto his shirt and onto the floor made ever worse by the alcohol in his system. The wounds looked truly ghastly and his lip was split in half down the middle and to the teeth. He grimaced and groaned as the pain began to set in and the adrenaline wore off.

Lisa had frozen on the spot with a look of disbelief at what she had done, and without saying a word to Mr Abdi or getting angry she went about her business whilst he writhed on the floor. She took a swig from the bottle of whisky to calm her nerves and grabbed the wad of cash off the table which she rammed straight into her bra. Next she went and grabbed her clutch bag and leather jacket from the other room, she was only gone a second and came back to look at Mr Abdi who was still curled over in pain and now spilling a substantial amount of fresh blood onto the floor and leaving fingers of crimson on the furniture from trying to pick himself up.

She stepped over him and rifled through the draws, in the bottom draw of his desk sat a small lockbox safe. The key was missing so she reached into the inside pocket of the jacket draped over his chair and produced the small key from inside. The box opened first time and inside sat neat bundled stacks of £50 notes. there must have been 10 grand there, all neatly in rows, she rammed it into her black clutch bag before kicking Mr Abdi one more time in the face for good measure then stormed out of the flat with no hesitation.

That night Lisa stayed with a friend in Shoreditch that no one from work knew about. She cried for a while and then she laughed. They stayed up and talked, taking cocaine and drinking wine, she told the story of what had happened, she also told her friend about the bag. She couldn't stay in London now, if Mr Abdi found her, she would disappear without a trace. She would need to leave at the earliest opportunity. When Mr Abdi was out of the hospital and sober he would surely be putting the word out to his distasteful little circle and before long Lisa would be caught, she could only imagine what they would do to her, it made her shudder just to think, whatever it was it wouldn't be quick. As they sat and told stories in the small Shoreditch flat Lisa looked up flights to Amsterdam, it was time to take a plunge.

Chapter 7: BA 430

Heathrow airport was always a stressful place, it brought with it the low-level underlying stress that seemed to linger in the air, the waiting and the uncomfortable white spaces played with people. It was always loud, and it was always busy it didn't matter what time you arrived, terminal 5 was the newest extension to the already sprawling space. A behemoth on the edge of the city that grew and hummed like a wasp's nest, the planes constantly circled in the sky waiting to land or to jet off in any number of directions. It was just before 9am and there was a freshness in the sky, there was no sun to see but the cloud cover was a light opaque grey and the air was still and cool.

James had checked in and sent his suitcase off into the unknown, security had been surprisingly painless and relatively quick and now he sat waiting for his gate to be called. In the spirit of the idea that he was doing his sort of detective adventure he had picked up 'A study in scarlet by Arthur Conan Doyle', the first Sherlock Holmes novel. It amused James to think that he would be going on any comparative adventure, in reality this was probably going to be a much-needed short weekend away in light of his recent circumstances. Hunting for the bag was simply a laughable fantasy that he had played out for himself.

Of course, he would still give it a go for no other reason than it would give him something to do whilst he wondered the streets and took in the sights. Perhaps he would hang out at some local café's, smoke with the tourists and wonder around canals through the red-light district. He had always liked Amsterdam, especially when he had been a little younger and much rougher around the edges. The place always seemed exciting and there was always somewhere to go and get lost in for a few hours. He was interested to see what would happen now he was slightly older and wiser, perhaps he would appreciate the city in a different light, seeing it through a different hue, it was far less about excess for him now and more about the appreciation of culture.

The would be detective looked up from his book to check the gate on one of the many screens that dotted the terminal, the plane was preparing to board, so he closed his novel and started to walk down towards gate 18 to board plane BA 430. When he arrived he was one of the last to board, he had arrived with plenty of time and the woman on the counter smiled warmly, greeted him and requested to see his passport and ticket one last time before he stepped off down the tunnel towards the door of the plane.

The plane itself was perhaps two thirds full and dotted with all kinds of interesting characters, you had the usual groups of young people off to smoke themselves into a haze, a surprising number of normal average joe types and the odd character that would catch his eye as he walked down the plane. The first was a stunning young woman with a black bob gazing out of the window, as he shuffled further down the plane a skinny man with swept back hair and another with a distinct violent scar sat chatting loudly with little regard for those around them and laughing at each other's crude jokes, closer to the back of the plane two very different men sat quietly reading. There was no reason for them to stand out, they looked like normal 30 something year old men reading quietly but something stood out, he couldn't put his finger on it.

The flight was over before it had even started, James managed to read almost half of his novel in the time and had put his headphones in to drown out the ambient noise of the people around him. Various passengers did the usual of ignoring the cabin crew at the other end and scrambled to collect their hand luggage from the overhead lockers whilst the cabin crew looked on in despair at the hordes of ignorance that unfolded at the end of every journey. James waited patiently, he was in no rush and in no time at all he was out of the plane and on his way to collect baggage.

David and Mike hadn't spoken much on the plane and instead had decided to read quietly, it wasn't that they didn't enjoy each other's company but that they didn't often get the chance to simply relax on the way to a job and so they had learnt over the years to make the most of these sorts of moments. They had gotten tickets near the back; it was another force of habit for them that allowed them to have eyes on everything that was happening in front of them. It wasn't that they were ever expecting anything to happen, but they just liked to know what was going on.

David had the details for the Audi Q7 that was waiting for them in the airport at the other end, it would be a quick turnaround after the flight, straight off the plane and to work. They had rung Elliot Wicks to warn him to return the bag, sometimes it didn't have to be an ordeal but clearly he had decided to ignore the message and had continued to run and now they had to hunt him down and retrieve the package. It was an inconvenience but at the end of the day it simply meant that they were being payed and so it was no real skin off their backs.

It was at Schiphol Airport in Amsterdam that the problems began for the pair. Once they had left the plane, as they walked from the plane towards the exit and the outside world a police officer stood with the customs official, sitting at his feet was a studious young beagle. Usually a dog like that would be sat sniffing for drugs, especially in Amsterdam but apparently not today, as the pair approached to walk past; the dog bolted into action and faced them excitedly before sitting proudly and looking up at Dave and Mike. The officer stood in front of them and put his hand out, another officer appeared from around the corner as if he had been hiding in waiting.

It was a bomb dog, trained to smell out minute amounts of explosives. David and Mike looked at each other and then to the officers in front of them, they had no choice really, they would have to go with them. They were escorted to a holding area and separated, after this they were both searched thoroughly and questioned, the whole process took several hours, several hours that they really didn't need to be spending sitting around for no good reason. They both knew they didn't have any explosives on them, and it took an eon of arguing with customs officials and showing security licences before it felt like progress was being made. The whole circus ended abruptly when a supervisor received a phone call from his office a few rooms away in the same department. They were let go quickly and without question, an officer rolled his eyes as they took their passports and left. It had been a waste of everyone's time, the beagle smiled to itself at a job well done.

Lisa had left the airport with no problems; she was very much hoping she wouldn't have to explain the huge amount of cash she was carrying in her baggage but luckily no one had stopped her to check. Outside she hailed a cab and began the relatively short journey into town, she had friends there, friends that she had met whilst working in London; other working girls who would be happy to see her and would certainly have her back. Lisa was turning up unannounced, but she was sure it would be ok and besides she hadn't had time to ring ahead and plan a relaxing trip away, she was there on business.

The taxi dropped her off near Amsterdam Central Station and she walked into the red-light district. The streets were narrow and alive, the aroma of skunk floated through the air and the stampedes of stoned patrons crammed the tight little spaces, the curious wondered around with them. Lisa got lost a couple of times in the twists and turns but eventually in a window directly on one of the canals she spotted her, Vonya Ivanova winked and waved to passing men, she wore nothing but red lingerie and she bathed in a red light behind a windowed door. She was tall slim and beautiful with deep brown hair that waved down past her petite shoulders, as with all the girls that worked Amsterdam, she wore too much makeup and kept a continuous smile. Lisa smiled to herself, she hadn't seen her friend in at least a year, they always stayed in touch though, the girls from Soho always stayed in touch.

Lisa swanned from down the pavement and into view standing outside the door and smiling to her friend, Vonya's face lit up at the sight of her and Lisa approached the door, Vonya cracked it open a little and poked her head out. 'Oh my god babe it's great to see you! I'm working, you know how it is can we meet up a little later?' Lisa produced some notes from a handbag she had slung across her body, 'how about you let me in for a good time then', she winked with a cheeky smile. Vonya ushered her inside, no one cared what happened as long as it was paid for. Once through the door and out of the eyes of the public the two hugged a tight warm embrace, 'what are you doing here'? Vonya asked with a beaming smile, 'I will tell you all about it in full detail later on, I left Mr Abdi, and I'm going rouge' she chuckled.

Colin and Simon hadn't really bothered to bring any luggage with them, they were more than happy to travel light and get anything they needed on the road, it was the nomadic life, a life they both embraced fully and had thrived within. Both men knew Amsterdam well, a staple part of any diet for those who indulged in excess and found it necessary to punish their bodies in search of volatile highs and brain numbing adventures.

Simon suggested the first point of call, there was some shopping to be done, essentials if you would, that made any kind of psychotic hunt run smoothly in his eyes. For such a shopping list there was only one-man worth speaking to and that would be Klaus Übel, the man was a legend in the local underground. A narcissistic bitter German who loitered in his attic surrounded by firearms and some of the best cocaine, speed and heroin Europe had to offer. The man was an urban fucking legend, untouched not out of fear but out of the fact he was respected as part of the furniture, he provided drugs and weapons to almost every major player, and he would happily arm both sides of any gang war as a neutral party and everyone in town knew it.

On the dirty streets Simon knew exactly where he was going, the pair walked shoulder to shoulder down the familiar alleys, people moved out of their way, they had an aura of insatiable violence and a swagger to their step. Klaus's house wasn't hard to find, it looked like every other house on the street but run down and bombed out on the outside. It stood out in stark comparison to the tall colourful buildings that surrounded it, some of the windows were cracked, the brickwork was bare, and the paint had peeled from the door. Rustic and worn out it had a quirky interest upon the narrow street engulfed with flowerboxes and cobbled roads.

Colin and Simon didn't have an appointment but Klaus knew Simon well so there would be no problems, plus he was no stranger to random drop ins when things went south in the gang wars of the Netherlands or West Germany. There was no doorbell so Simon banged the door loudly several times, a window slid open from several floors above and a shaggy, skinny pale face poked out looking down, 'fuck you Simon I was sleeping, I have a phone you know', Klaus smiled down with a wicked skeletal smile. 'Wait one minute I'll come and let you in', the window slid shut again and a few moments later the door flung open, Klaus welcomed them inside.

'So, what will it be gentlemen, business or pleasure'? he said this whilst hugging both of them like old friends, 'business today Klaus, we would like to see your toys please', Simon had a glint in his eyes. 'Maybe a bit of pleasure too', Colin jumped, he figured there was no point loading up and going on a wild rampage without something in the pocket to keep the senses alive and kicking, it simply made the whole thing into good sport and a bit of fun in his eyes. Klaus nodded to them both 'well come, with me then gentlemen, I have plenty of toys to play with', as he led them up the stairs towards his attic he lit a half smoked hash joint that had been behind his ear.

'So, how's business in London Simon, are you still doing the bikes'? Klaus asked as they reached the attic door, 'yeah business is alright mate, same old really... still riding of course, been doing a bunch of stuff with warehouse parties recently, the money's decent and most of the punters are harmless so it's easy going', Simon shrugged. Klaus swung open the door to his attic and grabbed several tatty suitcases from underneath tables, 'I think we'll start with these', he winked to them as he flipped open the first case. Inside sat various models of handguns and revolvers, mostly in good condition, almost all had probably been used before at some point, the variety was unreal.

Surprisingly Colin was the first to dive into the suitcase, a well maintained Colt 1911 had caught his eye, it was a reliable firearm and it was certainly intimidating, he raised it up closed one eye and pointed it towards the brick wall at the far end of the room before taking a closer look inspecting the piece and cocking it and looking at the working parts. 'How much Klaus'? Colin gestured to the handgun, 'That will be 400 euros, it comes with 3 magazines and because you're old friends I will throw in some ammo for free' Klaus stood on the far side of the room, arms crossed and continuing to smoke away at his joint slowly.

Simon looked through the stock but didn't seem satisfied, 'you got anything else… something with a bit more punch to it'? Klaus chuckled and walked over and produced another suitcase from under another table, 'of course Simon, an artist must always have the right tools for their craft, I just got something that will fit you like a glove', he was always a good salesman, much like a good tailor, he provided his service with style and panache. He flipped open the case and inside it sat a single weapon, a Winchester pump action shotgun, this was no normal pump action though, the butt had been sawn off and turned into a pistol grip and the barrel was sawn off as short as possible making it far easier to carry. A hole had been drilled through the grip and a lanyard had been attached. It was a particularly violent piece of kit. Simon fell in love. '600 euros all in with 50 shells, 40 buckshot and 10 solid slug for the big stuff...', Klaus already knew Simon would buy it. Simon brandished the shotgun with a grin and simply nodded in agreement.

Klaus could tell that Simon still had an appetite, 'anything else'? Klaus said as he was already rummaging through various boxes and bags. He clunked an old sports bag onto the table and unzipped it. Simon had placed his new shotgun to one side and began to rummage, he produced a razor-sharp machete from inside with glee 'I'll take it'. He placed it with his other new toy and rummaged some more, until he found something else a little special, a Japanese tanto fighting knife in a sheath, he slid it out and inspected the blade closely, it was sharp enough to split hairs, a work of art.

'Well I think that's me', Simon nodded happily with himself like a child in a sweet shop, 'would sir like a bag'? Klaus said in his best store managers voice, 'why yes please Klaus, leather if you have it', Klaus rummaged for a moment before retrieving a leather sports bag, worn but useable and it just fit everything inside perfectly. Colin jumped back into the conversation, 'there is one more thing, are you still selling that fantastic coke you used to have'? he posed the question with fond memories of snorting copious amounts off a hookers tits several years previous. 'Better!' Klaus announced, 'this stuff will blow your mind Col, just don't rack your usual lines, it even gave me a kicking the first time I did it... how much do you want'? Colin pondered for a moment before turning to Simon 'shall we get a half'? Simon shrugged 'fuck it', 'we'll get a half (half ounce) please Klaus and I think that should round it off nicely'.

Klaus gave them the drugs on the way back down. He kept that in a cabinet next to his office, the grand total for everything had come to just over 2 grand, not a bad price considering what they had come away with. They paid and stood around talking for a few minutes about parties from 10 years previous before they said their goodbyes and Colin and Simon were unleashed back out on to the cobbled streets more dangerous and ready to lock and load than ever before. They were a match in a fireworks factory itching to be lit.

Chapter 8: Four tabs of Shiva

It was a Friday afternoon, Eanna and Leah had the weekend off from work. Eanna worked in one of the various hostels dotted around the city welcoming travellers at a budget with the promise of good parties and cheap rooms, he had a kind round face with a dark trimmed beard. Today he was wearing his favourite Celtic t-shirt and a pair of shorts with black Adidas trainers and some fairly jazzy watermelon socks, he had a noticeable thick Irish accent and every few lines were dotted with witty one liners and observations. All in all, a good soul to be around and a seasoned wreck head with a passion for a good time and friendly people, he had lived in Amsterdam for almost 7 years now.

Leah was tall and slender with beautiful captivating eyes, she had long straight blonde hair which she almost always hid under a sports cap. The first thing people noticed was her distinctive and quirky dress sense, she wore a bright yellow Kill Bill crop top and a utility waistcoat with various pockets which were usually stuffed with lighters, cigarettes and god knows what else. She wore baggy cargo trousers again brandished with an alarming number of pockets and practical spaces. On her feet were a pair of Nike pumps, perfect for raving and jamming around town. Nothing on that outfit should have worked together and yet somehow Leah made it look cool. She worked in a coffee shop and looked incomplete without a joint in her mouth or being back strapped in her hands.

They sat in the Hill Street Blues, a coffee shop in the red-light district covered from floor to ceiling in graffiti and tags, it was a mecca for graffiti writers and sold some of the best weed Amsterdam had to offer. Eanna sat smoking a fairly chunky joint filled with kush, at his feet sat a black leather bag that contained his work clothes, wallet and a few other bits. The room was filled with the smoky mist of sweet-scented herb. Leah sat in a leather armchair skinning a joint from the same bag. 'So, what are we doing tonight I'm itching to go out like', Eanna said as he blew a plume of smoke into the basement of the iconic little café. 'Like I want to get fucked up but I want to have an experience tonight, like something a bit off the wall and all that', he sat back in his chair pondering and took a swig from the bottle of beer on the table.

Leah smiled with a wicked little glint in her eyes, the one you make when you're about to make the best kinds of bad life choices. She rummaged around in the various pockets on her utility waistcoat until she found what she was looking for and produced a small baggy held between two fingers. Inside the baggy sat four small pieces of colourful blotter paper connected like stamps, 'well how about this then', she said with an infectious grin. In her hand she held four tabs of Shiva acid, strong stuff that would send you sideways for anything up to 12 hours easily. If Eanna was looking for a different experience he was definitely going to get it.

Leah took the little sheet from inside the baggy and ripped it in half so they would have two each and passed it over to Eanna, he inspected the colourful little squares for a brief second before placing it on his tongue and closing his mouth and smiling back at her. 'Thanks, it's been a while, this'll be a laugh', Leah smiled back and placed her half onto her tongue then sat back to light her freshly rolled joint. The LSD would probably take about 45 minutes to kick in and from there the rollercoaster was going to speed up rapidly for the next 5 to 6 hours. The trick to a trip like that was to just ride it out and enjoy the experience, don't over think it and let your brain wonder, after the first 6 hours it would settle down into a mellow floating high that just rolled out into the distance.

They agreed to wait at the Hill Street Blues until the trip kicked in at which point, they would see where it took them, things were more interesting that way. Some time passed before Leah started feeling a glowing warm sensation in her chest, the first thing any tripper would realise is the feeling of ecstasy and joy and a physical glow in their body. Eanna looked down to see the table vibrate for a split second, the woodgrain seemed to flow and move freely, it would seem that the pairs adventure was truly about to begin. Leah looked out of the window where the colours of the outside became ever more intense and the clouds gently swirled into each other in a none threatening psychedelic dance.

It was time to step out into their brave new world and unleash their senses onto the exciting cascade of noise, colour, sounds and smells that awaited them. The streets swayed and faces distorted, as they walked the cobbles seemed to jump on the spot and the buildings that flanked the streets seemed to grow in size and loom down over them. Movement left trails of light behind it and it was as if they both felt they could float, they rolled into a few bars saying very little to each other but simply enjoying the moment, they didn't need to speak, everything was too beautiful. They ordered a few drinks on the journey to have an excuse to be there and smoked cigarettes and joints just to watch the smoke tumble and flicker into the ceiling, as the smoke dissipated the ceiling began to warp and distort in every direction.

Elliot Wicks stood at Klaus's battered doorstep and banged three times; it was getting into the evening but Klaus Übel was always open for business. It was like the man never slept, maybe that's why he looked so grey and dishevelled Elliot wondered. As usual Klaus pocked his head out of the window and peaked down to see who was waiting below, 'ah it's you, one second I will be right with you', the window slammed shut and a little while passed before the door swung open and Klaus welcomed him inside. 'You're a face I haven't seen in a little while, it would appear you're a wanted man Mr Wicks so please I do not wish to appear rude but the quicker you're gone the better', Elliot understood perfectly well and the comment confirmed his suspicions. his name was out. he would need to act quickly and get out of Amsterdam by the morning if he stood a chance in hell.

Up in the attic Klaus pulled out his signature worn out suitcases and opened them on the various tables around the room, 'I need something reliable, easy to carry and with a bit of stopping power', Elliot proposed to the salesman. Klaus pulled out a .38 Snub nose revolver and spun the cylinder much like something you would imagine from an old western. 'It is reliable, small, and you know about it when you've been hit', he cackled to himself as he said it, 'mmm... I don't know, it's only got 6 shots I was hoping for something that will keep me in the action a little longer if it comes to it', Elliot said as he scanned the cases in front of him. 'In which case I would suggest a Browning Hi Power 9mm, these things are everywhere and for good reason, its well-made, it uses 9mm which is easy to acquire and to be honest Elliot it looks cool too'.

Klaus placed the handgun in Elliot's hand who checked it over and played with the working parts for a while, 'yeah this will do, I will take it and 4 mags, I also need 200 rounds of ammo for it and a shoulder holster if you have one..', Elliot continued to inspect the weapon in depth as he said it. 'No problem lets saaay 600 for everything', Klaus always liked to make his clients feel like they were receiving a good deal. Elliot counted out the money in 50's and put it into Klaus's bony skeletal hands which then slid the money into the pocket of his worn-out Levi jeans.

'Do you mind if I load up here'? Elliot asked politely, 'sure, yeah crack on', Klaus waved him on. Elliot removed his jacket and fitted the holster, he had to take it off a few times to get the straps to the right level to feel comfortable. It was a lovely piece, worn in tan leather like something from an old cop movie, it looked cool for sure. As Elliot began to bomb up his magazines Klaus rolled a crude hash joint and lit it with a zippo in his pocket, the zippo was like something you would find in a tacky flea market and had a skull holding two revolvers on it, you would imagine a 13 year old owning it, yet it was fitting for someone like Klaus. The frail German offered Elliot some of the joint, he kindly refused, this was no time to start getting out of his head but one thing he could use was a drink.

Elliot left and thanked Klaus for his time, as he left the building, he made sure to look both ways to see if there was anyone around that might cause him a problem. The plan in his head was to stop in a local bar he used to know, have a quick drink and then move on, either steal a car to get out of town or jump on the next train out of there. He would keep moving as much as possible, paying cash only until he made it to Turkey, from Turkey he could hop on a plane to maybe Thailand or Vietnam and drop off the face of the earth a little bit easier. He hadn't ironed out the details, but it was the best he had been able to think of under the pressure and it got him out of immediate danger for sure.

A few minutes down the road he reached Suzie's bar, a notorious biker bar owned by the Hells Angels and a safe haven for cut throats and crooks from all walks of life. It was a shady traditional pub and surprisingly small on the inside but cosy and you could tuck yourself in a corner pretty easily and stay out of the way of any potential trouble. For such a rough place there was never trouble inside, people knew better. This was a safe space for dangerous people, old rock music usually played and in the toilet read the sign 'take drugs here and we will break your legs', a stark warning to the tourists that wondered through and thought they could act in Suzie's the same way they could act everywhere else.

Elliot ordered a pint of Heineken and sat at a table with his back to the wall, it wouldn't be sensible to stay there for too long so he sipped and enjoyed the ice cold pint but all the while worked out the final details of his plan in his head. He settled on taking a train out of the country that night, if he stole a car it could bring too much heat and he was already struggling with the heat he was under now. Play it cool he thought to himself, he wasn't up for taking any unnecessary risks that could bring everything crashing down on him.

Eanna and Leah laughed uncontrollably at a stuffed animal they had seen in the window a few shops back, it was dark now and they had truly peaked, the lights melted around them and everything breathed to a rhythm and pulse. They might as well have been walking on a distant alien planet, they were now very much in the swing of things and loving every moment. Eanna had been kicked out of one of the bars a few streets back when the bouncer found him stroking one of the lamps hanging from a table, it had been too beautiful not to touch, if the bouncer could see what he saw maybe he would have sympathised.

They stopped at a shady little pub on the corner and peered in from outside, 'this place is cool', Leah said, 'we should go in but we need to act cool it's a little rough round the edges in here', she said with a confirming nod. 'Yeah fuck it I could do with a beer', Eanna always enjoyed a cold beer on a trip, in fact he always enjoyed a cold beer, he wasn't an alcoholic he just liked beer. With a deep breath and a serious effort to straighten up they pushed the door open and slid inside. Once inside Leah grabbed a table next to a shady looking man who stared at a half-drunk pint of Heineken whilst Eanna got two drinks from the bar and paid. Eanna placed his leather bag down with his belongings inside and sat opposite Leah.

'Right what's the crack, I might head back to mine after this, want to come with and we can smoke a couple of joints and wind down'? it had been a fairly intense trip even by their standards and so Leah agreed. They sat in peace for about 5 minutes before they couldn't hold it in anymore, Leah had become fascinated with the wrinkles on the dishevelled old barmaids face and burst out laughing uncontrollably, everyone turned to look at the pair who were now bent over double howling at nothing, they had barely said a word since they arrived.

'Get the fuck out you fucking wasters', the barmaid growled over the counter, 'you have 30 seconds to leave before I slap the shit out of you little freaks', that was their cue to leave and they sprung to their feet clearly jumpy from the threat and under such warped conditions began to run, totally freaked out by the altercation. Eanna grabbed the black grip as he sprinted for the door. They must have kept running for a good 10 minutes, acid heightened the senses and the smallest of emotions could explode out of control if not properly managed. The fear passed now they had escaped the deadly sharp tongue of the old woman and they burst out laughing again.

Chapter 9: A chance encounter

James had booked into a dilapidated hotel near the station some hours before, he had felt restless and so decided to grab some food before starting to plan how he could go about finding the mystery thief with the bag. He wasn't exactly going to bump into him in the street and it's not like he had any local heavy hitting criminal connections to rely on for information. He thought back to the conversation he had with Charlotte several nights before. She had mentioned something to do with the gang having links to the diamond trade and drugs. He figured if anyone knew this guy was in town it would be someone from that world. He could maybe pose as a journalist looking for the latest scoop on the story. No, that was stupid, why would these people just talk to some random reporter? What if he tried to get in with some drug dealers? buy some stuff a couple of times and then bring the robbery up in casual conversation to see what happens? Again, a stupid idea with little real-world application. The whole thing seemed rather stupid now he had arrived.

Feeling down on his luck and unsure what to do James decided to walk along one of the quieter canals to enjoy the scenery and soak in the cool Amsterdam night, he slowly shuffled down the street with hands in pockets. If he couldn't think of a viable way to make progress by tomorrow, he would enjoy a few days in town before returning to London and arranging some interviews. It wouldn't be too hard to find work, James figured he would just bite his tongue and take what was available, these pipe dreams and escapades needed to stop.

He started to hear uncontrollable laughter from behind and looked over his shoulder to see who was causing the commotion. On one of the corners stood two figures, a man with a beard and a blonde woman in cargo trousers and wearing a cap. He smiled, they seemed to be having a good time, the man had a black bag slung over his shoulder. They tried to collect themselves and started walking the same direction. 'Evening, what's the crack? Having a good night'? The man said in a thick Irish accent, the woman seemed to become slightly distracted by a tree as she walked. 'I'm good thank you, you two seem to be having a good time I wish I'd found a good party', James replied.

'Yeah we've had a sick night, dropped acid earlier and been tripping around the red light district all evening, we just got kicked out of some bar so we're heading home now', Eanna pointed back in the direction they had come from. 'I'm Eanna and this is Leah', he held out his hand and James shook it, 'I'm James, nice to meet you', 'So James what brings you to Dam, good weed and pretty women I'm guessing'? The Irish man asked with a warm laugh. 'Actually, surprisingly no, it's a weird story I must admit', James paused for a second, did his new friends really want to know about a failed detective story in the making? Probably not, yet again it was someone to talk to and something to pass the time.

'Well you see there was recently a robbery in London, something big, a whole bunch of safe deposit boxes were nicked and well one of the thieves got away. Rumour has it that he ran away to Amsterdam to make his escape and well

I basically had nothing better to do and a sense of adventure so I figured that I might come out here to see if I could find the stolen goods for myself. The news said that whatever was stolen could be worth millions, it's all a bit stupid really, now I'm here I realise I don't actually have a clue what I'm doing'. James told the pair of his plight feeling slightly embarrassed to say it out loud as he did.

'That's sick'! Leah piped up for the first time, 'you should go to Suzie's bar there's loads of dodgy looking people in there, I bet you could find your thief inside', she said this with a twinkle in her eye and an abundance of enthusiasm. 'Yeah that's cool', Eanna said, 'a bit like one of those old detective novels or something huh, you should get a magnifying glass and a pipe then you'll look the part'. You could see Eanna picturing it in his head as he sized James up and down like an overzealous photographer on a fashion shoot.

'We're going to Köln in a few days to see my cousin', Eanna continued, 'He's got a sick little house there and the party scene is awesome, you should go check it out whilst you're in Europe, it doesn't take too long to get there on the trains from Central station'. The group had been walking down the quite canal for about 5 minutes and enjoying each other's company. James amused himself watching his new friends tripping and finding all sorts of mundane things truly fascinating. It was nice to forget everything else and just enjoy the moment for a little while, he never did that enough anymore. He made a mental note to make sure he enjoyed the little moments more in the future. James almost decided on the spot to ditch the whole idea of hunting the thief and just take a bunch of magic mushrooms in Vondelpark, the city was infectious for making you want to have a good time.

The trio reached a bright yellow door that sat just off the canal it opened up into a small square connected to a road on the far side, 'well James it's been a pleasure but this is us lad, maybe we'll see you again one day who knows, it's a small world', Eanna said as he fiddled to find a set of keys in his shorts. 'We're going to smoke a bit of weed and try to come back to planet earth I reckon, it's fun being a Martian but eventually you want to land the ship you know'? 'Yeah no worries it was nice meeting you guys I hope you enjoy the rest of your night, you've made me want to trip around Dam too', James chuckled as he waved them goodnight and kept walking. It was starting to get cold and so he slid his hands back into his pockets, Suzie's bar sounded interesting, perhaps he would go to check it out tomorrow.

From where he was James figured he could probably find his way back to the hotel which was another 5 minutes or so down the road, if worst came to worst he could use google maps. How people functioned before the internet was beyond him. This was especially strange to think seeing as he had grown up without smartphones and coped absolutely fine, it was no surprise everyone was glued to their phones these days it was extremely useful. He decided when he got to the hotel, he would brew a cup of tea and maybe watch a film on the dodgy little tv on the table in his room, a good plan indeed.

Chapter 10: It's gone

It took Elliot a few moments to realise what had just happened. He was exhausted and the whole scene unfolding had distracted him. He sat in his corner seat at Suzie's bar and had just witnessed two young party types totally off their faces get turfed out of the bar. They were lucky they left quickly because some of the patrons looked particularly rough tonight, especially the two sat at the far end of the bar. Elliot looked down and erupted into a state of panic, where was the grip bag? There was a bag sat near him, but it wasn't his. It was a truly gut-wrenching moment, how had he been so stupid to let his attention slip like that.

Elliot grabbed the other bag and bolted out of the bar as fast as he could, it must have been those freaks. What if it had all been a distraction to get the bag away from him? He had no idea which way they had gone, he sprinted down a random road in a distant hope he would catch them up ahead, they had been gone for 30 seconds tops, they couldn't have gotten far. 'Fuck'! he shouted, Elliot was at the end of his tether and the anger just poured out. He thought to himself, which way would they have gone? If he walked down towards the nearby canal it was dead quiet, no one would go that way, they would be too easy to spot. He decided to work his way into the heart of the red-light district.

He searched for a while but couldn't see anyone that matched the pair he had seen in the bar, they could be anywhere now, for the first time Elliot was truly on the verge of tears. He wasn't leaving without his retirement fund. There was a stone step just by him, he sat down for a second to think of his next move. He decided to look through the bag he had picked up at the same time. He unzipped it and peaked inside, a pair of jeans and a hoodie but sat on top was a leather wallet. Elliot breathed out a sigh at his first piece of good news, slowly he opened it up and examined the contents inside. Printed onto a driving licence was a gift from his guardian angel, the name Eanna Crehan and an address. If these guys had just tried to pull a fast one on him then they were fools. It was probably best to pay Mr Crehan a visit with his Browning Hi Power. Elliot made the decision to wait and watch a while, who knew, it could easily be a trap, he would recce the address for a few hours before he made his move.

Intel had suggested that Elliot used to drink in Suzie's bar, so David and Mike decided to pay it a little visit to get a feel for the place. After the ordeal at the airport that morning, the two professionals had collected an Audi Q7 from the airport carpark. Inside the boot lay a variety of equipment that they had requested from their fixer for the job. MP5K's with plenty of magazines, ammunition, a few thousand Euros in walking around money and their pistols, Walther P99's a good quality 9mm that had become popular in the security industry in recent years.

Intel had also suggested that Elliot might have been in contact with the legendary Klaus Übel, a well-known weapon and drugs dealer who just refused to die. It was best to avoid meddling with such a character firstly because he was essentially seen as neutral and on hallowed ground by the underworld and secondly because he was famous for not spilling information on anyone, ever. It was that quality that had gained him his reputation through the 90's and up to the present day. It was rumoured even European security services had approached him in the past to acquire weapons and ammunition for less than savoury operations that couldn't officially be put on the books. It was thought that this was how the German salesman was able to survive untouched.

David and Mike opened the door to Suzie's and stepped inside, their presence was very much felt. The bar was very used to dangerous people, but these guys came across as a more calculated kind of violent. It's one thing being willing to kill but being trained to kill is a very different kettle of fish. 'What can I get you boys'? the haggard old barmaid asked as they took their seats on the left side of the bar. 'I'll have a pint of any good lager please', David said, 'Mike what are you having'? Mike decided on a cider and so the pair sat as she poured the drinks and took in the atmosphere of the place. A few bikers hung around minding their own business. They were discussing a commotion a few minutes before; some drug freaks had run off and a well-dressed man who looked like he hadn't slept in days had left in a hurry.

The pints were poured, and the men paid in cash. Mike looked to his right, two men sat at the other end of the bar, one was a lanky man in a bomber jacket and slicked back dark hair, the other was short, stocky and had a distinctive scar down his face. He recognised them and tried to remember where from. It was the plane. He wondered what they were doing in Amsterdam? whatever it was it wasn't for a holiday. He had a gut feeling that there was just a small chance that they were all here for the same reason. Meanwhile David produced a picture of Elliot from his pocket.

'Excuse me mam... but you wouldn't have happened to have seen this man around would you'? He asked politely yet firmly. The Barmaid spun around and gave the two men daggers with her eyes, 'who are you? I don't talk to no police; you think you can come in here and just start asking questions'? She became defensive, this was no place for police, a safe haven for the rotten cores of society. 'No mam we're not police, just concerned friends, we think our friend might have been here', he continued to gently quiz the woman. 'I haven't seen nothing, now if you are police or something then get a warrant, you look like police, I should know I've seen enough!' she seemed nervous now, barking like a dog stuck with its back to the wall.

David apologised and returned to his drink; the way she had become more defensive once she had actually looked at the photograph made him feel like Elliot had been there. And if that was the case it must have been recently; they were most likely hot on his tail. It wouldn't take long to catch him; they had several local police officers on the payroll so any information that went through the police would come directly to them. Their client was well connected and they had plenty of resources at their disposal to get the job done, they didn't even care about a budget, it seemed they were willing to do anything to get the bag with the stolen goods back.

Two tequila shots appeared in front of them, 'from them two at the end of the bar', the barmaid nodded over to the shady characters from the plane who had stood up to leave. The shady men knocked back their shots, the one with the slick back hair winked at them and just like that they left. No one said a word to each other throughout the interaction, it would seem that David and Mike weren't the only people out for a hunt. This could get messy if they didn't finish the job soon, the more bodies they had to bury at the end the worse it would be for business and that simply wasn't their style, unless of course that was what the client requested, some had a flair for a violence and like any service they catered to their client the best they could.

Lisa walked down the dark streets, Vonya had set up a meeting for her with this crazy old German guy. A smart looking man burst out of a less than savoury, grotty little bar and sprinted past her, he looked panicked, maybe he had pissed someone off she thought. Lisa shrugged it off and continued on her way. The side street was barren until a few minutes later when she passed two hard looking men with military haircuts walking the opposite direction towards the bar, they looked like cops she thought. Again, Amsterdam could be a strange place and it was of little concern to her as long as she was left well alone. Vonya had said this German guy was called Klaus and sometimes he would book a few girls to stay with him for a day or two, sometimes he wouldn't even fuck them, they would just smoke hash and watch old horror films. She said he sold guns and was insistent that in light of recent events Lisa needed to protect herself.

She turned up to the shabby house and knocked on the door as she had been instructed, he knew to be expecting her. The window slid open and the grey face looked down, 'ah you must be Lisa... welcome', a minute later the door opened, and he welcomed her inside. 'Well I must say you are far more beautiful than my usual clients', he was complementary, yet he wasn't creepy. 'Thank you', she said in an attempt to be reserved. 'Follow me, I keep everything up here'. She followed him up to his raw brick attic and Klaus went about his usual process of sliding various suitcases out and placing them on tables for her to view his prized stock.

'Now madam tell me. How experienced are you with firearms'? he seemed genuinely interested as if to find her the perfect fit. 'Not very… I've shot a few times back home but I'm no expert I'll admit', she felt slightly out of her depth, but she didn't show it. 'Ok that's no problem, well in which case… I think you might suit something like the Walther PPK 7.65, it's not too big in the hands, it will put down a target without too much recoil and you could probably fit it in that lovely black clutch of yours', he rummaged through several bags before retrieving the pistol. 'Give it a hold and see how it feels', Klaus checked the chamber before handing it over to his customer.

Lisa clasped the grip and took a shooting stance, it made her feel powerful, she liked it, in all honesty he could have given her anything and she probably wouldn't have known much better. This guy seemed to be a genuine salesman, not some rip off artist, Vonya did say he was the best though to be fair, and she trusted Vonya on such matters. A small smile grew on her cherry red lips, she felt like a sexy killer from the movies and she liked it. No one was going to fuck with her, she was the boss now, after the glassing incident with Mr Abdi she had found a new confidence. The handgun was definitely adding to it.

Chapter 11: One hell of a comedown

Eanna was the first to wake up, to tell the truth they had barely gone to bed and he couldn't sleep properly. The acid had worn off and left nothing but a warm afterglow, he rolled out of bed and into the living room and adjoining kitchen. Leah lay asleep on the sofa in an awkward sprawled out pose with her cap over her face. He pulled a half smoked joint from the ashtray and lit it before turning the kettle on to make a coffee. The clock on the wall read 09:04, it was still early and Eanna didn't plan on doing much with his day, maybe pack ready for Köln. Leah rolled over and stretched to the sound of the kettle boiling behind her.

'Morning', she croaked as she sat up and extended her slender arms into the air, 'can you make me a coffee too'? she craned her neck round to face Eanna, 'Yeah course', he said. Leah then began to roll a fresh joint from the coffee table in front of her. The young stoners were planning on a mellow morning with no interruptions, perhaps a good film or whatever shit tv was on, it didn't matter, neither of them had slept particularly long and the afterglow of the LSD had put them in a relaxed mind frame, maybe they would muster up the energy for some breakfast in a bit.

'Have you seen my bag'? Eanna asked whilst lifting pillows and shifting objects around the room, 'yeah it's by the front door I think', Leah replied as she licked the rizla in her hands and checked her handy work. He walked over to the front door and looked perplexed at the bag on the floor for a second, 'this isn't my bag... what the fuck', he picked up a black grip bag that sat in front of him. It was a similar shape and black, but this looked more like a military style grip, much better quality and whatever was inside was about twice as heavy.

Leah lit the joint she had rolled as she kicked back on the sofa, behind her Eanna had unzipped the black grip bag and simply stared into it with an open mouth and a wide surprised look in his eyes. 'Leah... I think I picked up the wrong bag last night', he placed it on the sofa and showed Leah what was inside 'holy fuck!' she exclaimed, she leaned in to take a closer look, she had dropped the joint in the process and didn't even notice. They both stared into the black grip completely thrown by what they had seen. 'What do we do'? She asked, totally unsure how to even respond.

Smash! The front door to the flat came flying in and the man from the bar the previous night burst in gun in hand and a mean look on his face. Both of the stoners jumped out of their skin and flew backwards towards the far wall. Eanna held the grip bag in his arms almost like a shield to protect himself from his potential attacker. 'Give me the bag! Now!', he roared from across the room whilst aiming the gun directly at them. 'Give it to me now or I will paint the wall with your fucking brains and take it!' the man seemed serious, his eyes were cold and ready to kill.

Everyone stood in silence for a second, Eanna and Leah were stunned like rabbits in headlights unable to move and cowering against the far wall. 'Now!' the wild-eyed man shouted again, he waved the gun wildly at them and began to walk across the room towards them. Leah panicked and picked up a wine bottle from the windowsill next to her. Without hesitation she threw it, hitting the man square on the chin without breaking, it didn't knock him down, but it certainly diverted his attention for a moment. Leah had bought them some time, but she had also just ignited a chase, a chase the pair were totally unprepared for.

The window of the first-floor flat was open and a car sat parked below. Eanna grabbed Leah's arm and burst into action, 'fucking hell, jump'. He launched himself out of the window with the grip bag under his arm and landed on the roof of the car below. His weight dented the roof and the car alarm rang out in the street. Pedestrians stopped to witness the spectacle. Leah looked back on the crazed man who was regaining his focus and after hesitating slightly slid out of the window and dropped down onto the concaved car, denting it further and cracking the windshield. They began to run like they had never run before, Eanna didn't even have shoes on, he hadn't even noticed, the adrenaline was rushing through his veins. They took the first side road they could find and continued sprinting through burning lungs without stopping for a second.

David and Mike were walking - in no particular rush when it happened. They had been on their way to recruit a local police officer onto their books. It was common practice and easily done, especially when done subtly and with little risk to the other party. All they needed was a heads up if any information appeared that might relate to their case, no dirty work, just a simple phone call, very few people would refuse 1000 euros to make an odd phone call. There was an almighty crash and a car alarm rang out down the street around 30 meters in front of them. Two young crazy looking types sprinted past with sheer terror in their eyes, the whole thing was quite peculiar.

David looked up to the window that he thought they had just jumped from, the curtain fluttered outwards and danced in the street. The scene had a kind of comedic charm, pedestrians and traffic had stopped to witness the car below that bellowed out an alarm, the roof had caved in and a crack like lightning had appeared across the glass. Some laughed, others shook their heads at the hooliganism of the modern streets whilst others took out phones and began to film as one might have expected.

From the window appeared a head. A man leaning out and preparing to jump in pursuit of the stoners. It was Elliot Wicks! Everything clicked in an instant. David and Mike looked at each other in disbelief, the job had fallen right into their laps, 'go after those kids, I'll grab Elliot', David spat out as he began to charge in the direction of the building. It was at that moment David and Elliot's eyes met; Elliot's face switched from determined anger to pure fear in a single blink. He launched himself from the window and bolted in the opposite direction knocking over a man who had his phone out to film in the process, Elliot ran with gun in hand, pushing and weaving his way through the busy Amsterdam street.

David ran in pursuit, he had no reason to panic, he could do this all day, he would catch him eventually. 'There was no point running away you're just going to die tired', he thought to himself as he weaved through the same street in hot pursuit. Elliot skidded around a corner, peaking back as he went to see how close his pursuer was. Elliot didn't know who the man was, but he had a pretty strong feeling he didn't want to be his friend. He had the ex-military look, the kind of hired muscle with brains to go with it that only the right clients knew how to acquire. This new street was much quieter and so as David came around the corner Elliot fired several shots blindly behind him, neither came even close to their target but embedded in the wall off to the left.

Still he ran, his pursuer was closing in, the few people in the street now cowered in doorways at the gunshots, he fired again wildly hoping to hit the predator that closed him down. This round fell short and bounced off the floor and ricocheted in some random direction. It was a narrow street with no turnings until it opened onto a main high street area about 40 meters ahead. Elliot crashed through the front door of a small restaurant and into the kitchen again shoving and barging his way through anything that got in his way.

People shouted as pots and pans came crashing down. David was hot on his tail now and was planning to double tap Elliot in the back of the knee at the first opportunity he got, what would he do with him afterwards though? The car was parked at least 3 or 4 streets away and driving around here was a nightmare. Elliot narrowly made it through the fire exit into the next adjacent street without David grabbing him, Elliot could hear him breathing and the sound of his footsteps behind him, it was getting desperate. As he sprinted down the new alley like street, he made one last effort to turn around and hit his attacker with a stray bullet just before the street opened up a few meters ahead.

Before Elliot could even turn to raise his handgun and shoot, David had already stopped, bladed off, drawn his weapon from under his jacket and fired two perfectly placed rounds into Elliot's knee. It was surgical precision performed with lighting speed, over in well under a second. Elliot dropped to the floor as if someone had cut the strings on a puppet and David was on top of him in a flash, he kicked Elliot's handgun away and it skidded a few meters out in front of them. David looked around to see who was watching the commotion, most people had darted into any corner to get away from the shooting yet one woman walked right past them, headphones in, oblivious to anything around her or simply too thick to care.

Mike had gone after the two stoners. He didn't know how yet but they must be involved somehow. Once he found them it wouldn't take long to find out. He had noticed the grip bag under the bearded man's arm, could that be the bag they were there for? Quite possibly. Mike turned the corner but couldn't immediately see the kids up ahead, he knew they must have come this way because people stared down the street bemused by the two freaks they had just seen running for their lives, one of them without shoes. Several gunshots rang out in the distance, 'fuck that must be David', Mike thought to himself and decided it would be better to call off the chase for the stoners for now.

He darted back to the car which wasn't too far away and climbed into the driver's seat, the engine roared and the tyres screeched as the car launched into action. Mike hurtled in the general direction of the gunshots he had heard. He had to take a slightly strange route away from the canal and north up to the next main road. Another couple of shots rang out. As Mike hit the main road, he came into traffic, he leant on the horn and mounted the pavement. People scattered as he drove the car a few meters down before diving off the curb and back into the road. The car skidded around a stationary vehicle and down the wrong side into oncoming traffic.

Two shots sounded so quickly that it could have sounded like one to the untrained ear, it was really close like it had come from the next street. Mike pulled up to the narrow side street and stuttered to a halt as the ABS kicked in, as predicted he had got it right. David stood over Elliot Wicks with his handgun drawn and pointing towards his head.

Elliot bled from the leg but seemed conscious and alive. Mike left the engine running and got out of the car to cover his partner with his weapon. The whole ordeal had taken less than a minute. David produced some handcuffs from a pocket in his jacket and slapped them onto Elliot's wrists, picked up Elliot's gun and lifted him into the back seat of the Q7 and got in the back with him.

'What happened to those kids'? David asked as he stepped in, Mike jumped back in the driver's seat and sped off and out of town, 'they shot off into the red light district, I don't think they'll be hard to find, I heard gunshots so figured we would focus on the main target', Mike swerved traffic and checked both directions before running a red light. 'Yeah fair enough mate, thanks I wasn't sure what I was going to do with this prick once he started shooting up the street', David had applied a tourniquet above the knee on the thigh and was placing a gag in Elliot's mouth and preparing a black bag for his head.

'The rounds have both gone through the knee, he'll be ok, I don't reckon he'll bleed out on us', David inspected the bullet wounds and applied a field dressing, he had ripped back Elliot's trousers to reach the wound. He was no use to them dead yet, there was valuable information to be had. In the distance sirens could be heard arriving at the scene, the whole thing had happened so quickly that all the parties involved had gotten away before a single officer could arrive. Mike thought about how many people had just potentially filmed the whole thing on their phones. The last thing they needed was a gun fight in the middle of the day to appear on YouTube, it was already going to be all over the national news for sure.

The shadow black Audi Q7 drove for around 40 minutes until it was clear of the city and into the industrial district, they would need to ditch and burn the car as soon as possible, the handler could deliver a new one no problem. It was also probably a good time to phone to update the client. They would probably be happy to hear that Elliot Wicks was under control, the bag wouldn't be far away, a little torture would reveal its location. The car had calmed down, there was no reason for aggressive driving once they had made it clear of the scene. Under his hood Elliot could be heard groaning, the men ignored it and allowed him to continue, they had both been shot before and could appreciate it did hurt a bit.

They slowed down and pulled into an abandoned old warehouse complex, the place was more rust than metal and some of the units looked like they hadn't been used in a very long time. The furthest unit on the left was empty so the car pulled up to the side out of sight from the main road and the engine cut out. David and Mike got out in unison, Elliot was pulled by the scruff of his jacket and semi dragged hobbling into the building. Inside was dark, Mike flicked a switch and the buzz of rows of halogen lamps sounded out followed by plinking noises as some of them flickered and flashed into life. There was a leak somewhere because a pool of stagnant water loitered in a corner and a consistent dripping could be heard echoing in the distance. Sun light perforated through holes in the ceiling where rust had eaten away the metal structure.

Elliot was dragged onto a chair in the centre of the expansive room, David uncuffed him and then cable tied all four limbs to the solid piece of furniture that had been left by the previous owners many years before. Once tied down, Mike went back outside, opened the main large doors and drove the Audi inside before closing them again. Next to the chair was a battered wooden table. David removed Elliot's black hood but kept the gag in his mouth, while this happened Mike returned with a rolled-up leather satchel from the boot of the car, laid it on the table and opened it. Inside were various tools, a hammer, pliers, scalpels a saw and various knives. Elliot began to cry to himself; this certainly wasn't going to end well for him.

The professionals left Elliot alone with the tools and walked away to allow him to contemplate his future. David pulled out a burner phone and typed a number he had memorised into the keypad. 'Good morning, I think we've made some good progress…. Well for a start we have Mr Wicks in custody, we're about to start the interrogation now… yes we'll make sure of it, no problem we'll deal with him, he won't darken your door again… we haven't got the bag, we think it's been lifted but we have some good leads, will keep you updated.. speak soon', David put down the phone and nodded to Mike, they had their orders, Elliot's day was about to get a whole lot worse.

Mike had already sent another message to the handler, a new car would be arriving at a supermarket carpark not far from their current location in roughly 2 hours, that gave them time to work at the job at hand. Mike walked over to the selection of tools on the table, he had put some leather gloves on and ran his hand along his little collection. David stood in front of the terrified thief. 'Mr Wicks, you have stolen from some very nasty people, we are here to enact their will, if you do not answer my questions in full and in good time… you will feel pain like you have never felt before.. now before we begin do you have anything you want to say'? David removed the gag and tilted his head as if to listen. Elliot knew that nothing he did or said would change anything and so he sobbed, he sobbed in despair and prayed that whatever was about to happen was quick and swift.

Mike had found his tool, as he ran his hand to the end of the formidable list of torture weapons, he reached a bunch of sewing needles threaded into the fabric of the satchel. He pulled them from the bag and with no words and no emotion placed one just under Elliot's right thumbnail. Next using the pair of pliers, he slowly forced it under the nail, he had to use his other hand to hold the thumb in place to stop Elliot pulling away. Through the crying and the screams Elliot begged for them to stop. They hadn't even asked a question yet; but this wasn't about getting information. This was a lesson.

The nail turned bright red with blood under the surface and it raised away from the skin. Once the job was done, the end of the sewing needle protruded out of the thumb. Elliot had started to sweat buckets and he was pale, of course he had already been shot twice today as well. David stepped forward and calmly asked his first question, 'so I will get straight to the point Mr Wicks, where are the safe deposit boxes you stole'? Before he even had a chance to respond Mike pounced at him with another sewing needle and his pliers, this one he did slower and into the index finger of the right hand. Elliot snarled and screamed through clenched teeth, as it finished, he spat and spluttered.

'What's your answer'? David snapped, Elliot's head rolled back and he breathed heavily for a second before realigning his eyes with his torturers, 'the goods were in a b-b-b-black grip bag, I I don't have it, it-t-t was stolen last night, I swear…. I know who has it I have a n-n-name I'll tell you everything please just stop, I beg you', 'good', David replied before giving a look to Mike who was waiting in the wings. The third sewing needle was no better than the last two, this time his middle finger. The same gargles and screams and writhing in his chair, the same cold, calm look on the men's faces stood over him.

'Eanna Crehan! Eanna Crehan!... you saw me at his address this morning, there's a girl too, blonde... tall, I don't know her name!' Elliot Wicks wanted it to end, he was hoping that someone would put a bullet between his eyes but neither of the men pulled out a gun, they just stood, blank faced. 'His wallet is in my pocket, take it, he has the bag, I swear, I'm sorry! I'm sorry!' Elliot wept, the tears rolled down his face, this was not how he had seen it ending. Yet through the tears he accepted his fate and looked up to the angels of death, they controlled how he died. David leant down and began to release Elliot from the chair, he started with the hands which he put back into handcuffs.

'Thank you for your cooperation Mr Wicks', David said as he cut the cable ties on his legs and lifted him up from the chair. Mike had emptied two kit bags from the car and had started packing away his tools. David dragged and supported Elliot back to the vehicle and helped him get inside. Elliot wondered where they were going to take him next, why hadn't they killed him yet? David closed the passenger door and then locked the car before walking out of sight. When he returned, he was holding a water bottle, he opened the front door quite casually and then squirted it onto Elliot's face and body.

It was petrol! Elliot writhed and screamed, kicking at anything he thought would break to let him out with his hands still cuffed behind his back. David dropped the rest of the bottle in the back seat-well and with not a second thought lit a match. The first one snapped in his hand, all the while Elliot headbutted and kicked at the glass. 'NO NO NO!' he howled. The second match lit and David threw it onto Elliot's lap, he was engulfed in rolling flames immediately and the writhing became more violent than before, in just a few seconds the whole car was bursting into flames and Elliot could be heard inside screaming the last vicious, miserable breaths of his life. The smell of burning flesh and car filled the warehouse. The smoke billowed out in a thick black cloud. The two men grabbed their kit bags and left the warehouse to history. They had a new car to collect.

Chapter 12: Mugshots

Vonya shuffled into the sitting room of her one bedroom flat wearing a fluffy pink dressing gown with no makeup on and her hair tied up. 'Lisa wake up you need to see this', she flicked the news on with the remote. Lisa sat up from the sofa and pulled the covers back. 'What is it babe, what time is it'? The news was in Dutch, but Lisa could catch the drift of it from the images. Pixelated footage showed chaos on the streets of Amsterdam, a man being chased down back streets, guns drawn, and shots being fired. The same mugshot that had appeared on Mr Abdi's desk popped up on the screen as well as a young bearded man and a blonde woman and two bad quality pixelated pictures from the CCTV of two other men in boots with short hair. All wanted in connection with a gun fight in town. The news then showed CCTV footage from the Chiswick raid. It was all connected, whatever had happened downtown was something to do with the stolen goods.

Lisa lit a cigarette from the table, Vonya sat down and joined her, they sat watching the live news coverage, Vonya spoke good Dutch and so she translated the early reports from speculative journalists. The newsreader delivered the story 'The police are yet to make a statement. Several streets had been closed off with tape and officers in order for a full investigation to take place. Witnesses had said multiple gunshots had been heard as well as several parties running in separate directions. An Audi Q7 was also seen fleeing the scene, it was believed one of the suspects may have been shot in the incident, but police were yet to confirm the details.' A telephone number also appeared on the screen and a plea was put out for any witnesses or anyone with any information to come forward.

Her Walther PPK sat on the kitchen counter in the other room, she began to get ready to go to work, Lisa would need to follow up on this and see what she could find out about these new faces as soon as possible. In the bathroom she washed her face and reapplied a little bit of eyeshadow and mascara, she threw on some practical clothes and a flatter pair of shoes, some black trainers that still complimented her figure, most things did really. The handgun slipped into her handbag, she also had a spare magazine to go with it, she wasn't planning on having to use it too much so that's all she decided to carry. Besides getting into full blown gun battles wasn't really her style, beauty was her weapon after all, why threaten when you could just as easily seduce.

James had come to the conclusion that the detective game wasn't for him, he sat in one of the many coffee shops and was slowly working through his first joint in a very long time. He had forgotten what it felt like to get stoned, some of the other patrons gave him strange looks as he sat back with the joint between his fingers wearing his favourite lounge suit, the jacket was hung up and the sleeves of his shirt were rolled up. He had finished his book from the plane that morning and so he just enjoyed people watching. The coffee shop brought such a diverse crowd of people, young and old, the hip and the frightfully normal, he wondered where he fit into the spectrum. He was unsure if he could even finish the whole thing in one go and so put it down in the ashtray for a short while and ordered a can of coke to his table. His mouth was bone dry and his eyes felt cloudy, his head was light.

A tv on the wall played footage of some chase or shootout in town that morning, he paid little attention to it and simply allowed his mind to wonder. But the news didn't seem to stop, his eyes were drawn back to it again and again, of course he didn't have a clue what any of it said, he didn't speak a word of Dutch. What happened next would change the course of James's journey in a single moment. Eanna and Leah's faces flashed onto the screen alongside a mugshot of a 30 something year old man and two pixilated figures from the footage. He leant forward in disbelief, it couldn't be, what had they done? Those two hadn't exactly come across as criminal masterminds.

When the footage from the Chiswick robbery came on everything clicked, they must have taken the bag. He remembered the bag Eanna had the night before, had they even realised what they had? Leah really wasn't joking when she said you could find a thief in Suzie's bar. It may have come from complete chance with zero skill, but the job was back on, the universe had decided that James wasn't done trying to be a detective just yet. He stood up before his coke even arrived at the table, abandoned the joint and put on his jacket. It was only when he stood up that he realised just how stoned he was. These were not ideal working conditions.

The first thing to do was retrace his steps from the other night, in his current state it would be hopeless to try and work it out from where he was so instead James walked back to the hotel to try and figure it out from there. Once at the hotel he tried to recreate the walk he had taken the night before, he had done a massive loop, but he could remember the canal he had met his friends on. It turned out to be easier to find than he expected seeing as a huge cordon had been set up, a major investigation was underway and everything for several streets surrounding the house with the yellow door was closed off. James walked up to the tape to get a better view.

A police officer stood guard to ensure nobody came any further than the tape, inside the tape was a hive of activity. One officer took photographs, the car still sat under the window with its roof caved in and its cracked glass. Other officers wearing gloves stood in rows combing the streets for evidence of the gun fight that had taken place. Any piece of evidence was marked, other objects were being put into plastic bags. A few men in suits coordinated the investigation. Another officer could be seen up in the first floor of the flat taking fingerprints from the window frame. It became clear in that moment that this investigation was a big deal and that not only was half of the criminal underworld looking for the stolen goods but now the police were hot on the trail.

Were Eanna and Leah still going to Köln? James asked himself, one thing was for sure, either they would hand themselves into the first police officer they could find to clear their names, or they would escape Amsterdam by any means they could find. James's only lead at this point was to assume that they had done the latter and escaped to Germany, it seemed plausible. Whatever the outcome, James was back in the game, he actually knew who had the bag now, he had names, an address and he knew there was a cousin in Köln. Even if they didn't turn up in Köln, he could still find the cousin and try to make contact.

He decided to make his move now, if he was quick, he might even beat them to the city. He walked briskly back to his hotel, packed his belongings and checked out. Whilst on his way to the station he checked train times, it would take roughly 4 hours with two changes, the next train left in half an hour. It wasn't bad, he had a bit of time, so he got a burger in the station and waited. The excitement had returned, for the first time he wasn't on the back foot, he actually might be on top at that moment. He knew where they might be heading and no one else did. It may have been down to total chance, but James still felt like he had accomplished something deep down inside.

Whilst he ate his food and waited for the train to pull in, he considered the other men that were seen at the location, they had firearms, the whole thing was becoming very real. He considered that once he was known to be involved, he would be in a lot of danger. He had learnt how to shoot at Sandhurst, but it wasn't exactly world class marksmanship and what was the point knowing how to shoot if he didn't even have a gun. The only way he could make it work was to totally blindside the other people involved, never appear on anyone's radar, simply acquire what he had come for and disappear. Talk to no one without good reason, maybe stop using his cards and get a new phone. James began to plan how he could go dark and get away with it. It was almost time to go.

Chapter 13: The Greenhouse

A young man with a short beard and dreadlocks slowly swept the Greenhouse coffee shop, Frank Sinatra played in the background as he swayed with the broom. The evening had rolled in and dusk filled the street outside, the tables were clean, the machines had been drained and the chairs were flipped up onto the tables. All he had to do was finish sweeping and then do the mopping, the tills had been counted and his supervisor had left him with the key to lock up at the end of the evening. The coffee shop had been alive with the buzz of the incident on the news all day, things like this didn't happen too often, well not that publicly anyway.

The young man finished his work for the day. He put away the mop and switched off the lights to leave and picked up his rucksack from the back room. Before leaving he gave the place one final check over to make sure everything was ready for the morning and then went to the front door. He turned the key slowly, the lock always got jammed, you needed to get the technique right. The lock clicked and he pulled it open to walk out. Before the young man could even take a step, Simon appeared from out of nowhere, he placed a thick rough hand on the young man's chest and walked with him back into the shop. The man was too shocked to do anything and simply walked backwards with his hands up as sign of compliance.

Colin followed in behind him, he checked that no one had taken any interest in their activities before closing the door again and turning the key in the lock, he placed the key in his pocket. Still in a state of shock the young man scratched his dreadlocked head whilst keeping the other in the air 'sorry we're closed', the whole situation was very odd to say the least. Simon ignored him and took one of the chairs from a table and sat down. He placed his leather bag on the floor next to him. 'I will have a coffee please', he said in a surprisingly polite tone, as he said it, he pulled his tanto blade from his jacket and jammed it into the table picking at the grain of the cheap wood with the tip of the precision knife.

The young man obliged, he now knew exactly where he stood and walked half frozen back behind the counter and turned the machine back on. Whilst this was happening Colin leant up against the counter relaxed and simply inspected his fingernails. It took several minutes for the machine to even warm up, for this whole period no one said a word, they stayed in their positions in total silence, the coffee machine was the only noise in the room. It was surreal, it was strange, and it would have made a fantastic painting. The barista shook uncontrollably behind his silver machine, he dropped the mug and it smashed on the floor. Still he said nothing, took a deep breath and tried again. This time was ok, he filled the cup, placed it on a saucer and walked over to the table.

A second later he returned with a small jug of milk and a pot of sugar cubes. Simon dropped one cube of brown sugar in and stirred, he looked deep into the eyes of the young man whilst he did this, he didn't even blink. The young man stood very still awaiting the verdict of his work. He had the look as if he was a school child waiting to be sent to see the head teacher for some major infringement. Unsure what to expect a fear bred out of the unknown rather than the inevitable. It was the moment of truth; Simon blew the steam from his cup and whilst still holding the formidable knife in the other hand took his first loud sip of coffee. He placed the cup back on the saucer, looked off to the side and nodded very slowly in consideration.

'That's a good coffee, what is it'? he said in a forced voice like he was pretending to be some sort of gentrified connoisseur. 'iiit's from Camberley Coffee Club, they're new', the young man said in a timid voice, still he waited to attention in front of Simon who took a second sip. 'Its rich but not too overpowering… a nice aroma and aftertaste, you said it was called Camberley…', his words trailed off. 'Camberley Coffee Club, some British guy makes it', the young man stuttered. Simon nodded to himself again and went back to his coffee whilst paying little attention to the person stood in front of him.

Colin took a few steps from the counter and put his arm warmly around the young man's shoulder as if an old friend, 'you are probably wondering why we are here', the hippy was clearly nervous. 'I'm guessing you're not here for coffee, is it something to do with Leah'? 'Yes… Yes, it is something to do with Leah, well done, she does work here doesn't she'? Colin walked around the coffee shop; he kept the young man in tow. 'I already told the police everything I knew earlier', he said, slowly becoming accustomed to the presence of his new patrons. 'Well you see we ain't the police, we don't want to see your friend come to any harm so any information would be greatly appreciated…'. The young man contemplated for a moment.

'I can give you her address its written in the staff book in the office, honestly I have no idea what she's got herself involved in... do you know? The police wouldn't tell me anything, I swear I have no idea', he pointed towards a door off to one side where the book with her address was kept. 'Tell you what, what's your name'? Colin paused midsentence, 'Ricky... my names Ricky', the young man replied. 'Well Ricky why don't you get me that book and then we'll be out of your hair how about that'? Colin released Ricky's shoulders and pointed him to the door.

Whilst he rummaged in the office Colin racked three lines of coke out on the table Simon was sat at and rolled a note up. Simon took his first, as Ricky walked back with an A4 notebook Colin snorted his, he then took the book from Ricky's hands and passed him the note. The young man shrugged and took the line, perhaps it would calm his nerves a little. He rose back up surprised at the strength of the gear, it was good stuff, purer than what was normally found on the streets. 'Good stuff huh'? Colin looked up from the book with a smile. He flicked through the book until he found the page with the name Leah Deacon written in it and an address and phone number scrawled underneath.

Colin ripped the page clean out, that was all they would need to keep on the trail, he believed Ricky, it didn't seem like he would know anything valuable. He folded the ripped page and slid it into his bomber jacket pocket. 'Thank you for your help Ricky, you have been most valuable, now you can leave', Colin gestured to the door. Ricky froze back up again, unsure what to do or how to react, he soon realised he had little choice in the matter and grabbed his bag and walked to the door. Colin remembered that he had locked it on the way in and put the key back in and struggled to turn it, they both stood over the lock for an eon until it eventually budged. As the hippy left, he looked over his shoulder still very much bemused by the ordeal. 'Right I think we can be off then, no doubt he will be on the phone to the police any minute', Colin rolled his eyes.

'Very well', Simon said. He took a final swig of his coffee and slammed the cup back on the table before unzipping his bag and producing a small green petrol canister. He unscrewed the top and began to fling the potent liquid onto tables and across the wooden floor. 'What are you doing that for'? Colin asked puzzled. 'Just a little fun', Simon replied as he threw the canister at the far wall. He picked up his leather bag and pulled a cigarette from his pocket. He lit the cigarette and savoured the smoke in his mouth, he took a few more deep drags and blew on the glowing cheery before flicking it into the petrol which immediately ignited and began to spread around the coffee shop. The two men left with no hesitation. The fire alarm rang out and echoed down the street. The coke had kicked in, they felt untouchable, they swaggered down the street cigarettes in their mouths and ready for the next round of action.

Chapter 14: A seductive nature

Lisa needed to capitalise on the situation, whatever happened that morning was important and if she wanted to get the bag, she needed to find more information. There was no point getting big and bad, it wasn't her style and at the end of the day she wasn't the most intimidating person to look at. She had a different set of skills that she knew how to put to use very well. By the evening the police had reduced the cordon to just include the alley where the shooting had taken place and the area directly outside the house with the yellow door. She had hovered around for a while taking the scene in and generally staying out of sight. A lone policeman stood outside the yellow door preventing anyone undesirable making their way inside to tamper with evidence.

She saw an opportunity, he was young, fresh to the job, with eager eyes. She thought to herself that he was easy prey, she stayed off to the side out of view and inspected him for a short while, he had no wedding ring, not that it mattered half the time. As a young woman passed, he subtly checked her out in the corner of his eye, he certainly wasn't gay either, he was prime real estate. Lisa had found her target.

She removed her leather jacket to reveal her full figure in her knee length dress and sprayed herself with perfume from her clutch bag. The perfume bottle rested next to the handgun that sat idly awaiting its opportunity to be used. It was time to go to work, she came into view with a wiggle in her step. She knew exactly how to get his attention and as he spotted her, she gave him a wicked cheeky little smile, her eyes glistened in the evening sunset. As she approached, she played with her hair just a little bit. Lisa very much had his full attention.

'Hi, how's it going? I like your uniform', Lisa looked him up and down with her seductive eyes. The young officer beamed a grin, he clearly wasn't used to such attractive attention. 'You look pretty stunning yourself, my names Levi', he sparked interest in a strong Dutch accent. 'Well Levi, why don't you tell me what time you finish work and you can take me for a drink'. As she said it, she wrote her number down on a scrap of paper she pulled from her bag, underneath she wrote her name and a single kiss. 'My names Lisa', she added before he could get a word in. 'Yeah sure well I finish at 10, I can meet you at a bar in town around 11'. The young officer could barely contain his smile, he couldn't believe his luck. '11 it is… call me', with that Lisa walked off making sure that he could take in her tight figure and perfect round ass and thighs as she strutted away.

It was almost too easy she thought to herself, now it was time to prepare. Back at Vonya's she got ready, it was like the old days, but this time was on her terms. She slid into some sexy lingerie and picked out a revealing dress, something that said she wanted action but wasn't overly slutty. Subtlety was always key, it made them chase you. She put on fresh makeup and made sure her hair was perfect. Her and Vonya drank wine and took a little bit of coke that she had hidden away in a draw. Lisa looked stunning, she was going to turn heads and blow minds. As expected, Levi rang her as soon as he finished his shift and suggested a bar in town, somewhere nice with good drinks and food if she was hungry.

The last thing Lisa did before stepping out the door was take two pairs of handcuffs from Vonya's room and place them in her clutch bag. She also removed the handgun; she wasn't going to be needing that tonight. She spent the walk to the bar thinking about what kinds of subtle questions she could ask to get the answers she needed. The sooner she could get Levi out of the bar and into the bedroom the better, that's where she would really be able to break him down. There wasn't a man on earth she couldn't break in her hands with the most gentle of touches.

Once at the bar Lisa laughed at his jokes, flirted and fluttered her eyes. She wasn't overly attracted to him but that didn't really matter. She had a white wine and he had a beer. She told him she was a dancer just over from London on holiday. Levi had been in the police for a year and had a degree in art history. He was polite and smiled a lot, his jokes were cringeworthy, but she laughed anyway. He must have felt on top of the world. Before long she stood up and leant over close to his ear and whispered. 'Perhaps we should go back to your place', it was more of a statement than a question. He agreed, obviously.

They left the bar and walked through town like young lovers, she stopped him on one of the bridges and kissed him in front of the canal. At that moment she had his heart in her hand, he had barely known her for an hour and yet he had completely fallen for her. Lisa took him by the hand and the pair walked romantically back to his house, at the door she kissed him again. The second he opened the door she kicked in with the passion and pushed him against the wall. Lisa bit his neck and ran her hand down the outside of his thigh, he bit her lip and felt her shape with his hands before grabbing her ass and picking her up, she wrapped her legs around him. They kissed passionately in the corridor.

They eventually made it upstairs and she unzipped her dress in front of him to reveal the stunning body wrapped in lingerie below. He removed his shirt and threw her on the bed, from there everything became far more heated. In a paused moment she asked her first question, it was subtle. 'So, what were you doing protecting that house Mr Officer'? she asked whilst straddling her prey and running his hand down onto her supple breasts. 'Well I was protecting the scene of the crime, the house belonged to one of the kids that we're looking for, he got away with the blonde girl this morning', he said this and took off Lisa's bra then sat up and kissed her chest.

It was at this point that Lisa employed her handcuffs, her clutch bag was on the bed and so whilst his face was buried in her breasts, she produced the first pair and handcuffed it to Levi's right hand. He paused and gave her a look, she gave a wicked smile back that made him submit, she pushed him back and attached the other half of the cuff to the corner of his bed. She grabbed the other handcuff and before attaching it to his left hand, slid her warm crotch up towards his face. He bit his own lip in anticipation as she attached the hand to the other corner of the bed.

She rubbed herself against him, 'where do you think they ran to Mr Officer? Are you going to catch them and give them a... punishment'? at the word punishment she slid her hand into his trousers and slowly massaged his hard cock whilst looking him dead in the eye. This teasing began to tip Levi over the edge he was under her spell completely. 'Well the detectives think they ran away to Köln for some reason, the German police will probably find them' he stuttered with a shortness of breath. That was what Lisa had come for, she debated in her own mind for a second what to do with Levi who sat helpless below her horny and hard. Today she felt cruel, the handcuffs were the real deal and wouldn't break any time soon.

Lisa jumped off the enchanted man and quickly got dressed, 'where are you going'? he asked confused. She said nothing and simply slipped back into her outfit, she grabbed the clutch from the bed and blew Levi a kiss before walking out of the room. A moment later she came back in, Levi still lay dazed and totally confused by the situation, Lisa grabbed his police cap she had spotted sitting on the side, put it on and left again, looking over her shoulder seductively as she did. It took Levi a few moments to actually realise that he was now handcuffed to a bed with no keys. As she closed the front door behind her, she could hear him beginning to struggle to break free from upstairs. She giggled to herself and threw the police cap in the canal as she walked home, she hoped he didn't live alone. Surely someone would come looking for him when he didn't show up to work the next day. She rang Vonya, 'babe I might need to borrow your car', she then dropped the phone into the canal in a nonchalant manner as she walked with a cat like swagger back to the flat.

James boarded his train and immediately went to work on his phone, he had no name for Eanna's cousin, he pondered how to find them. Facebook seemed the best point of call, he brought it up on his smartphone and typed the name Eanna into the search bar. The screen flooded with Irish men young and old, there was no way he could find him in that mess, so he tried another approach. He narrowed the search by adding Amsterdam to the city location. He crossed his fingers that Eanna kept Facebook up to date, after all it seemed like he had lived there for a while. The phone seemed to spend an age loading; the signal was weak. He waited, the trees and building whipped past outside and the train gently rocked as it picked up speed and hurtled out of Amsterdam and towards Germany, there would be a change in about 40 minutes.

Eventually he got signal again and a few faces flashed up on the screen, second down he found his man. A smiling figure holding a beer with a few friends, a happy soul, he couldn't imagine this person on the run with stolen goods belonging to heavy Russian criminals. James clicked the profile and went to the section that said family, there was nothing there. It looked like he would have to go through Eanna's friends list individually, the last name was Crehan so that was the first point of reference. He hoped they shared a last name; it would make life much easier.

In just a few minutes James had struck gold, a young man, much thinner than Eanna. In his picture he wore a bright red Hawaiian shirt and a straw hat, he had the same smile. Noah Crehan, aged 23, lived in Köln. Now the next step would be to find an address, that could prove to be slightly more difficult but certainly not impossible. He had his work added to his account, Quest Software. James was starting to build a picture of who Noah was, he could work with that. James decided that he would find the address for Noah's work and go from there. He would wait for Noah to finish work and then follow him home.

The buzz felt unreal, this is what James had been looking for. He felt like a real detective, he was going to follow someone and then go on a stake out, it didn't get much better than that. It was everything he had been chasing, perhaps he was chasing the high more than he was chasing the wealth. There was no doubt the police would have made the same connection and would have made contact with Noah in some form or another. James had to be careful and keep himself out of sight and out of trouble, everything had become very real. It wasn't a fantasy anymore; he was living it. He took down the address for Quest Software and then spent the rest of the journey before the change looking at the blurred lines of shape and colour flying past his window.

Chapter 15: Breaking and entering

Colin removed the torn piece of paper with Leah's address on it and checked it against the door in front of him. 'It looks like this is the place', Colin and Simon both slipped on leather gloves, a staple part of any crooks' outfit. Colin had always been good with locks, he looked at the door handle briefly before taking a key from his pocket, it had 5 identical teeth in it much like a house key but more uniformed. Next, he took the back of a flathead screwdriver and tapped the key in the lock a few times, whilst doing this he kept the pressure on with his thumb to force the key to turn in the lock. After a few swift taps it swung round, it was an old trick that worked well with most house locks, it wasn't the first time he had bumped a lock in his time.

Both men moved into the place quickly and closed the door quietly behind them, they didn't know if Leah lived alone. If they weren't alone, they would need to subdue whoever else was at home quickly. It didn't look like the police had come around to search the house yet which Colin found surprising. This needed to be a quick operation, it was very possible that they were being watched by a surveillance unit outside. Now that things had gotten heated the paranoia had begun to set in. It wasn't a bad thing; it sharpened the senses.

It didn't seem like anyone was in and the lights were all off, both men started in the kitchen on the ground floor. Simon looked through draws that were filled with random papers and letters. Most of them were bills and junk mail that had simply never been thrown away. Meanwhile Colin observed the subtle details, he pulled a picture from the fridge, it was Eanna and Leah smiling at a party. Colin looked at the photograph and slipped it into his pocket. As he withdrew his hand from his pocket, he felt the large bag of drugs he had placed there the previous day and figured now was as good a time as any.

He pulled it out and poured some onto the kitchen counter, these lines were fairly insane, he had definitely misjudged this one. 'Perhaps it would be best to do those once they had found what they were looking for', he thought to himself. He took the rolled up note out and placed it with the lines ready to rock and roll. With that he returned to the job at hand, Simon had walked through to the next room and could be heard rummaging through whatever he had found. As Colin continued to inspect the kitchen, he spotted the calendar on a cork pinboard on the wall. In big letters in sharpie and circled in red was the writing 'Köln with Eanna'. He pondered if they could be that stupid, perhaps they were, from what he had gathered the stoners had made no attempt to cover their tracks and seemed pretty sloppy to say the least.

'Simon, I found it, I reckon we can go', Colin called through to the other room. 'Alright one sec mate', Simon called back. Simon took his time coming back from the other room. The first thing he noticed was the smell, and then he noticed the smoke lingering through the space. Confused he poked his head around the corner to witness the room erupting into flames, Simon stood in the middle throwing a fresh petrol canister around like a jubilant child.

'For fuck sake Simon, where do you keep getting all this petrol from'? Colin snarled. Simon simply shrugged and smiled, the smoke grew out of control and began to fill the whole house with a thick black choking cloud. They coughed their way into the kitchen.

'Simon... coke', Colin said muffled through his sleeve as he covered his face, through the black smoke Simon took his line on the kitchen counter and immediately broke into a violent cough, Colin then took his turn. They left through the back door, this time they were less subtle and simply booted it open. It crashed open making a cat bolt for its life and the two oxygen starved men stumbled out coughing their lungs out, the black rolling smoke followed them and tumbled into the sky. Simon was single-handedly responsible for keeping the whole Amsterdam fire service employed that night. Two huge fires were now ripping through buildings on opposite ends of the red-light district, both had a common factor, Leah. It was safe to say she would be in the spotlight for criminals and the law for some time to come.

There was no reason to hang around now, it looked like they were going to Köln, they would work out the details in a bit but right now they needed to get away from the scene. They climbed over a wall near the back door that connected into a small alley and the next street, it was like a small brick maze, perfect for getting away. And with that it was as if it had never happened, they both removed their gloves and walked through the streets pinging on a fresh high. It was time to go to Suzie's bar and plan, they could sit in the corner and work out what to do. The stoners would be easy to find they were amateurs at best.

David and Mike had picked up their new car after the information gathering that had taken place in the warehouse. It was a new Audi S8, it was probably best to avoid another

Q7, the police would be looking for one of those. The S8 was a good car, it was spacious and had plenty of boot space, it was also packing some serious heat with 571 bhp, it certainly shifted. It was dark now. They had spent the day pulling in various contacts and connections, both men sat with a Burger King on their laps in a shop carpark illuminated by orange streetlights. There were a few cars dotted around but little movement.

Mike held one of the various burner phones to his ear, he was talking notes in his notebook whilst he listened to the voice on the other end. He finished the conversation with a thank you and then turned to David to debrief. 'That was our friend in the Amsterdam police, no sign of Eanna Crehan yet, the girls name is Leah Deacon, apparently her house has just burst into flames. I doubt it was a coincidence. The police intel suggests that they might be trying to escape to Germany, potentially Köln. I suppose our main focus should be getting the bag before it falls into police hands or whoever else is closing in on it'. David finished chewing the bite of his burger before replying.

'We're definitely not the only people trying to get their hands on the bag and the police are all over it now, this whole job is turning into a ball ache, remind me to stop answering phone calls from Russians', they both chuckled as they finished off their meals. Mike tapped Köln into the satnav, it took its time to load and plot the route. 2 hours and 50 minutes in a virtual straight-line darting south east down the A2 and onto the autobahn. David collected the rubbish and went to put it in a bin about 20 feet away, once back in the car they looked to each other. 'Suppose we ought to get shifting then' he said as he turned on the engine. The car growled as they pulled out of the parking spot and into the road.

Eanna and Leah sat in a friend's house and panicked, Eanna had the key to the house to feed the cats whilst they were on holiday. They had been hiding there for several hours, the news played on repeat and their faces flashed up every time the story played. Leah paced up and down the room chain smoking cigarettes, she had broken into tears several times. Eanna sat on the sofa head in hands watching the news over and over again. His leg twitched with a nervous rhythm as he took it all in. 'What are we going to do Leah'? he asked with a broken voice. The bag sat on the floor in the middle of the room. 'Do we go to the police and explain what happened'? Leah asked, 'but what if they just lock us up thinking were involved, those men had fucking guns, they mean business', Eanna took a cigarette from the packet in his pocket and lit it. The cat sat next to him on the sofa unconcerned with what was happening.

They both hovered in the space, smoking anxiously wondering what to do. 'We need to ditch our phones', Eanna blurted out. 'If those guys are serious they'll be able to track us or something, like on all the police programs', Eanna took his phone out of his pocket, he had hundreds of missed calls and messages from friends and co-workers who had seen his face on the news. Leah looked at her phone for the first time too. They removed their sim cards and threw the phones in the bin. Then the news updated. 'Multiple fires had been reported in Amsterdam one at a house to the west of the red light district, the other was reportedly at The Greenhouse coffee shop, both fires were being treated as suspicious and may be related to the dramatic events early in the day', the news reporter read with a straight unfaltering face.

Leah burst into tears again, 'they're going to kill us Eanna, that was my work and my house… they're looking for us... I'm scared', Eanna also shed a subtle tear but he didn't want to admit it, so he hid his face in his hands for a moment until he felt it had passed. 'Well we need to think about what we're going to do... the longer we stay here the more danger we're in I think', Eanna stood up and rubbed his face, 'to be honest Leah I say fuck 'em, we should keep the bag if were already in over our heads, let's get out of town, go to my cousin and work it out from there, all I know is we can't stay here', Eanna put his case forward as he also paced around the room.

Leah thought for a moment and lit yet another cigarette, it was a rather surreal situation for either of them to be in. 'Well we will need to change our clothes, our outfits are all over the news and you don't even have shoes, do you reckon we could steal some stuff off your friend'? She walked through to the bedroom and started looking through draws, she changed into a t-shirt that was lying around and threw a black hoodie over the top. She kept the cap and put the hood up, 'what do you think'? she came back through and showed off the outfit to Eanna. 'Yeah I think you would pass with that', Eanna followed suit and went through to the bedroom and picked out a grey tracksuit, he also took some socks and a pair of blue running shoes that lay by the bed, they weren't a perfect fit but it was close enough.

They threw their original clothes into a rucksack and took any food they could find lying around, a few tins and the beers from the fridge. When going on the run a road beer always helped calm the nerves, well they assumed it might help anyway. 'So, we go to the station, we get on the first train to Köln, we go to Noah's and then get the fuck away from anywhere and wait it out with the bag, agreed'? Eanna listed off the loose plan. 'Yeah, I guess what else are we meant to do'? Leah replied unconvinced but trustingly.

Before leaving, Eanna wrote a note apologising to his friend for stealing the clothes and shoes, he also opened the box of cat food and poured the whole thing out into the bowl until it spilt over onto the floor. He was sure that considering the situation his friend would understand and forgive him, with that they left the house behind.

Chapter 16: Cold blooded killers

By the time James's train pulled into Köln the late evening had rolled in, it was overcast, and the moon was hidden away. He booked into the closest hotel he could find that wasn't too expensive and bedded down for the night. In the morning he would go to the Quest Software offices to find Noah. He figured if he hung around nearby then eventually, he would spot him leaving and could follow him to his home address. If he didn't show up, then maybe he could pose as a new foreign client and ring the company and see if he could find out why he wasn't in that day. Unfortunately, James couldn't speak German, so his options were limited. Something didn't sit right with this plan though. He already knew the net was closing in and that Noah was going to be a person of interest for any other parties that were involving themselves in this scheme, never mind the police.

A new plan, he needed to act tonight, it was still only around 9 o'clock and the office wasn't too far away from where he was staying, maybe a 20-minute walk tops. Perhaps it was time to do something truly daring. Up to this point James had been little more than a tourist of crime, following the murderous trail of greed and wealth into Europe. If he wanted to have a stake in the game, he needed to stop cheering from the side-lines and start acting. He removed his overly smart attire and threw on some jeans and trainers with a hoodie that he had brought in his bag but not touched, this was no time to stand out in a crowd, he had a plan and it was daring to say the least.

He left the hotel, hood up and nervous, his heart pounded at the excitement of it all. He was going to break into Noah's office. All of the worst-case scenarios played through his head, he could see himself being led out in handcuffs as he walked down the cool roads of Köln with his hands tucked into his hoodie. He didn't even know how he would get in, surely there would be an alarm or something, or perhaps an unsuspecting guard that he would need to evade. The walk seemed to take a lifetime and James payed little attention to the scenery around him, he was too focused on the task that awaited him. Köln was meant to be a beautiful city but right now he failed to see it, his vision was blinkered.

The office building looked like any other average space, it was a cube, five stories high and uninteresting from the outside. Several company names sat in placards on the outside, Quest Software was situated on the second floor according to the weathered plastic sign. James sat on a bench on the opposite side of the road for a while, there were still lights on around the building and a few cleaners could be seen working their way around various floors. It even seemed like there were office workers in some of the other parts of the building, probably catching up with late deadlines or important company projects. The windows lined up with the main staircase and he could see people if they were leaving from the upper floors.

A young woman looked as if she was leaving, a bag on her back and a navy-blue coat on. This was his chance, without even thinking it through James crossed the road, trying his best to time his arrival at the door with the woman's.

It worked, she reached the main glass door which required a card to enter and opened it to leave, as she did, she held the door for him to enter. He tried to have an air of natural confidence in the situation like he belonged there, he smiled to her as he entered to say thank you whilst being careful not to speak and give away the fact he was in fact English.

Once inside his heart beat ferociously in his chest, the adrenaline shot through him at a million miles an hour. He walked up the bland stairs to the second floor where the Quest Software office was based. Once he reached the top of the stairs, he encountered his second piece of luck, a cleaner had wedged open the main door which allowed him to walk straight in, a hoover could be heard droning around the space. There were perhaps 20 desks in the room all together, a relaxed office space with birthday cards on desks and mascots on top of computer screens. A sofa island and a coffee machine acted like an oasis in the small ocean of coffee stained carpets and rows of desks.

James threw a casual wave up to the cleaner, she waved back and continued with her job. He had relaxed a little bit as he settled into the role and slowly walked between desks looking for any sign of Noah's desk. He felt like he might have found it and sat down on the leather swivel chair. The giveaway was an Irish flag that protruded from the top of his computer screen, how many Irish programmers would be working for a company that small? Not many he reckoned. The next step would be to find Noah's home address, he scanned the desk for any useful information. There was nothing out but work notes and so he moved on to the draws, he had struck gold, sitting at the top of the first draw was a payslip with a home address.

He folded it up neatly and slid it into his back pocket, he had found what he came for and so he left the building as quickly as possible trying desperately to look like he wasn't running away. The rush was unreal, that moment had been what he came on the journey for, James breathed a deep sigh of relief as he walked away down the road with his hood up. There was no time to return to the hotel, he needed to look up the address on his phone and get there as soon as possible. Eanna and Leah would no doubt be arriving at Noah's house sooner or later and if they didn't then well at least he had his next source.

It would be a half an hour walk to the address and so James decided to hail a cab that was passing by. There was a hotel directly opposite Noah's house. A cheap bed and breakfast, the kind of place that was decorated by little old ladies and full of floral furniture and smelt of dust. He made a snap decision to get a room, the rest of his belongings were in his room by the station, but he could go back for them later. Right now, he couldn't afford to miss an important moment. James took a chair and sat in the window with the lights off, he could observe everything that was happening in the street below, yet he was almost impossible to spot, merely a shape in a dark room.

Outside had become quite and the road was barren and empty, the occasional dogwalker pottered slowly or someone might pass with hands in pockets on their way home from meeting friends. The silence was occasionally broken by the sound of a car swooshing across the scene, the headlights casting a shadow as it disappeared into the distance. A few houses still had lights on but for the most part people had gone to bed, a cat prowled the pavement looking for a night-time meal, James basked in the tranquillity of the quiet street.

Noah's house sat almost directly opposite James's window. He could see a light on inside which he assumed would either be the bedroom or the living room. Other than where he lived and where he worked James pretty much knew nothing about the man. He wondered if he had a family? what he did in his spare time? was he aware of his cousins' plight yet? There was no doubt that either a police officer or some criminal connection would be arriving sooner or later. It was reaching around 11 O'clock and James's eyes were growing tired, he kept himself busy by watching a solitary leaf dancing on the opposite side of the road in a light breeze. His other game was to see if the occasional cars would runover a can that sat ajar in the middle of the road.

His ears pricked up slightly, he sat up in his chair. Two men approached from the left, they had a different movement to their step, they were little more than shadows of figures dressed all in black. They moved with purpose and speed, yet they did not run or appear to be panicked. There were no distinguishable features, just two silhouettes wearing black clothes and raincoats. James was expecting them to continue walking as they reached Noah's door, but they stopped. The first man produced a crowbar from under his jacket and went to work on the door, it flung open with a pop and a crack as the wood from the frame shattered.

The second man watched his back, once the door was open, they both entered the house at speed. James could have sworn he saw one of them produce a submachine gun from under his jacket as he walked inside, it looked like an MP5K or something similar. He watched in stunned silence, another light in the house flicked on, there were a few seconds of silence and then a scream was cut off mid breath. The distinct sound of gunfire rang out and echoed down the street, it wasn't simply a few rounds but what sounded like a whole magazine of automatic fire unleashed in a single direction. As it happened the muzzle flash could be seen through the windows on the first floor of the cosy little house.

The two men left the house calmly and turned down the next road to the left, a few moments later a car engine started, and the screeching of car tyres could be heard as the roar of an engine faded into   the distance. Neighbours flicked on lights and poked heads out of windows at the violent racket. A few wondered into the street in dressing gowns and peculiar choices of footwear, all looked confused and hovered around Noah's front door.

Before long police cars and an ambulance arrived, the street filled with the flicker of blue lights and was a now a hive of activity. The police started to reassure, and interview concerned people, a tape barrier was erected, and paramedics tried in vain to perform some kind of miracle inside the house. James sat for almost a full hour simply watching the scene below, he had gotten to the lead first, yet it had been rubbed out with the single pull of a trigger. Noah was dead.

Chapter 17: The tunnel

By the time Eanna and Leah reached Köln it was pitch black, the train journey had been intense and nerve wrecking. Every police officer they saw filled them with terror, random travellers looked like hitmen and gangsters that were sat ready to gun them down on sight. Eanna clutched the black grip tight for the whole journey. It had slowly settled in that their lives would never be the same again, neither of them had said a word on the journey into Germany. They sat wondering if they would ever see home again and if they would ever laugh with their friends in bars and cafés after what they had witnessed.

Köln was quiet. As they stepped out of the central station the gothic cathedral loomed over the pair. It was beautiful and intimidating all in one, like the situation they found themselves in it was overbearing and truly epic. The lights from the historic structure cast great shadows that created deep contrasts in its intricate stonework designs. It was said that up to 3000 people had died making it, the sacrifice of human life in order to create something that would be seen through the ages. When taken into perspective, a human life was cheap. If a stone building was worth 3000 then how much was the bag worth? Probably plenty more than had already probably paid in blood.

The two stoners walked down towards the river Rhine to take an underpass underneath the station, they had been trying to stay as low profile as possible, using different entrances and exits, avoiding cameras where possible and taking the long route to their destination. They were no experts, but it seemed like a good idea to take some precautions. Near the base of the tunnel the homeless hung out drinking, a junkie pushed a needle between their toes on a small green verge. It was not the place to hang around too long, graffiti littered the walls around the mouth to the tunnel and a pungent smell of urine took over. It may have been a beautiful city, but it had a septic underside that was gracefully ignored.

They walked into the tunnel; it must have been 30 meters long with a single flickering streetlamp in the middle. It was an unnerving place that gripped people as they walked through, most locals avoided it if possible, there were easier routes around to the other side. Along one wall boxes and sleeping bags marked the sleeping spots of the local vagrants. To Eanna and Leah's surprise there were cars parked along the other wall. It would seem illogical to park a vehicle in what was so obviously a shady place. Overhead a pigeon flapped around between the metal beams that held the station up above them.

As they walked a figure appeared out of the shadows up ahead and stood as a stencilled silhouette in the end of the tunnel. The two stoners kept their heads down and walked towards the human shape. Eanna gripped the bag ever tighter, it was probably just another junkie. It was when they heard the footsteps closing in behind them that they really started to worry, these weren't just the footsteps of another wanderer but someone deliberately closing them down. They reached roughly the centre of the tunnel when a thick Manchurian accent called out from behind them, 'Eanna and Leah I'm assuming'? they both turned around to meet the voice and simply froze on the spot unable to talk or move for the fear that had washed over them.

They didn't know who the man was, but they knew exactly what he wanted. 'My colleague and I have been trying very hard to track the two of you', Colin stepped towards the pair slowly and loosely, a wild drug fuelled look in his eyes and a gun in his hand. Behind them they heard the distinct sound of a pump action shotgun being pumped and made ready to fire. Eanna and Leah simply held hands and stayed frozen, this was not the people that they were, they had no wish for any involvement in violence.

Colin could see it in their eyes even in the shadowy and dimly lit tunnel, 'I'm not going to lie kids, we were going to kill you in this tunnel, but I will make a deal with you… I'm assuming that is the bag we are looking for'? Colin pointed to the black grip with his handgun, Eanna looked down to it and then nodded nervously back to Colin. 'Well in that case, I will make you a deal, hand me that bag right now… and we will let you live, you run off and you never look back', Colin said it solemnly and seriously. Footsteps grew louder from the other man that boxed them into the tight little tunnel, it felt like the walls were shrinking in on them.

Eanna didn't need to think twice, there was nothing worth losing his life over and so he took a few steps towards Colin and gently put the bag down in front of him before walking backwards and re-joining Leah's side. Colin slipped the pistol into his waistband in the small of his back and knelt to inspect the contents. The two stoners could feel the shotgun behind them, ready to explode at the first sign of a wrong step. Colin unzipped the black grip and looked inside, he paused for a moment to take in what he was looking at, a smile grew on his face and his eyes glowed, this was definitely what they had been looking for.

With that he stood up, now with bag in hand. 'I suppose you two can leave then', he waved Eanna and Leah to go back the way they had come. With no hesitation they scurried out of the tunnel and back into the tranquil night and the looming cathedral, they disappeared into the distance lucky to be alive. Colin had turned to look down the tunnel to witness the kids sneaking off into the distance whilst probably thanking god for the first time in their lives at the fact they had actually just saved their skin.

Simon stood behind him, his demeaner had changed and his eyes had squinted. He stared soullessly into Colins back. From under his jacket he raised his now cocked sawn off shotgun and pointed it directly at the back of Colins head. Colin clocked on to what was happening and didn't dare move, if he did, he knew exactly what Simon would do to him. He gripped the bag tight and stood very still whilst pretending not to notice. 'I suggest you drop the bag Colin', Simon said with a wicked grin. 'Why are you doing this'? Colin asked without letting up his grip. 'Because I can Colin, because I can', Simon aligned his shot and made sure it was centred on the back of Colins head. He felt no remorse, he didn't really care, in fact it had been the plan all along. Simon had been waiting for the right moment to take Colin out for a while.

Slowly Simon began to squeeze the trigger, he could feel the pressure under his finger. The shotgun was about to go off in his hands, in front of him Colin had shut his eyes, there was nothing he could do and nowhere he could run or hide, he had fallen into Simon's dirty trap, he should have known better than to trust him. Bang! A round went off and a body crumpled to the floor. Colin jumped on the spot; he couldn't work out why he wasn't dead. Claret and fragments of skull and brain speckled the back of his head. He turned around to see Simon collapsed in a heap in the road behind him, the shotgun lay in the arms of the folded body.

Colin was still confused, a stunning woman walked towards him wearing all black and holding a gun, as she came level with Simon, she let off two more shots into his solid frame, 'give me the bag', she said. She only said it once, Colin threw the bag down in her direction and raised his arms in surrender. The whole situation had become rather surreal for him. He wasn't particularly scared; the years of coke had numbed the senses to a point he could function rather well under pressure regardless of the outbursts of violent anger every so often. He waited to see what the next move would be.

They stood face to face about 10 feet apart, Lisa held all the cards. Colin stood with his arms raised in silence. She raised the gun to aim in between his eyes, he wasn't having a good day, they stood, the moment lasted forever. You could have cut the tension with a knife, every little sound amplified, it was the most intense moment that no one would ever see. She blew him a kiss with her cherry red lips and pulled the trigger of the handgun. Click, she pulled it again, click, click. It only took a second, but it was enough. The gun had jammed, and Colin was bolting for the exit of the tunnel. He made it around the corner just as Lisa worked out to pull the slide to eject the blocked round. It fell to the floor and she let out another shot as he dashed around the corner.

She picked up the grip and looked around for witnesses, Lisa stepped around Simon's mutilated body and swaggered out of the opposite side of the tunnel, no doubt someone had heard the gunshots and the police would soon be on their way. She made it out the other side and into the road that opened up slightly. Lisa stepped into a red VW Polo she had borrowed from her friend Vonya and changed the plates, another trick she had picked up working for Mr Abdi back in the day. She threw the bag onto the passenger seat next to her and turned on the engine. She had got what she had come for, there was no reason for her to stay. It was time to get out of the country and to start a new life. First things first though Lisa thought that perhaps she should lay low somewhere for a while and have a little holiday, she had certainly earnt it. With that thought she pulled out of her parking space and drove into the night, the police cars flashed past her on her way out of town. Without another thought she was gone.

Chapter 18: An alliance of sorts

It was long past midnight, but James still sat and watched out of the window into the street, the police had removed Noah's body now, he had watched the body bag being loaded onto the ambulance. The street had died down slightly but detectives still worked hard within the house, a man photographed the street meticulously. Neighbours had been interviewed and dates for them to go to police stations had been arranged, most of the lights in the street had turned off again. Only a few police cars remained, and the cordon had been pulled back to just tape up the area immediately in front of Noah's front door.

James didn't watch the scene simply out of curiosity, he had reasoning behind it. Eanna and Leah surely had no way of knowing about the gruesome murder yet, this meant there were two potential options. The first was that Eanna and Leah had met a similar fate and currently sat lifeless in a ditch somewhere filled with holes or the second was they were still on their way to the house as he waited, fully unaware of the horrific death inside the address. He had no choice but to assume it was the second option and so he waited patiently. He hoped that they would arrive soon because his eyes were tired, and he was losing his concentration rapidly.

The time passed ever slower, the boredom consumed him, the only entertainment was the police officers who went about their work below. He pulled a cigarette from the box in his pocket, he hadn't realised how long it had been since his last one, he was careful to lean away from the window when he lit it. No one was aware of his presence there and he intended to keep it that way. He took a large drag from the cigarette and blew it into the room, he was fairly sure it was no smoking room, but he would deal with that issue later, right now he needed his fix.

It was 2.38, perhaps he should go to bed he thought, he argued with himself as to what was the right thing to do. If he didn't take his opportunity there and then he might lose it and he would never get the bag, he needed to be patient. Now that he had started smoking, the second he finished one he lit another straight afterwards. He would sit up all night if he had to, it wasn't like he didn't have anywhere to sleep when the time came. His eyes were heavy, and he had to fight his head nodding back in his chair, it was a struggle, but James managed it, he stood up for a moment to regain his composure.

Two people walked down the road towards Noah's house, they were hard to make out but distinct in the dark street. One wore a grey tracksuit, the other looked like a young woman wearing a hoodie. They paused for a moment near the front door and then kept walking. James sat forward taking great interest in the pair, why did they pause? Was it them? His gut told him that it was Eanna and Leah, they had a similar bounce and they looked too interested in the address whilst shifting along with hoods up to not be involved. He was surprised the detectives hadn't noticed them.

James grabbed his hoodie and ran out of his hotel room, he burst down the corridor and jumped down the stairs, he made it into the street in seconds. He still hadn't gotten his arms into the jacket and so he adjusted himself as he tried to look natural whilst going in the same direction as the two people, he thought he was trying to catch. It had to be them he was sure of it, he walked quickly down the main road, he had lost sight of them but there was no way they could have gotten far.

He got to the first side road and glanced to his left; there they were. Their pace had quickened, they weren't running but they certainly weren't hanging around. James took the turning and followed suit, as he walked, he sped up to try and catch up with them. There were still police around and he didn't want to be seen running down the road at such an ungodly hour. The officers hadn't noticed them and so he was able to close the gap quickly, when he got close the stoners spotted him and began to run. 'Wait, wait it's me, James from Amsterdam! I don't want to hurt you', he called down the road. They were a considerable distance from the murder scene by that point.

Leah turned to look at him, Eanna stopped a few steps ahead. 'You guys need to listen to me, you're in a lot of danger... Eanna I'm sorry to say this but your cousin Noah is dead'. Eanna leant up against the wall and clutched his head in his hands. Leah spoke up, 'how did you find us'? she glared at him with distrust. 'When I saw you on the news I realised that you had the bag I was looking for, after that I took a gamble, I knew you were planning on coming to Köln and figured it was the best chance I had of finding you, I looked up Eanna's cousin and found his address through his work, then it was a waiting game... I don't know who killed him, but I do know they looked like serious guys... I'm sorry that you've been dragged into all this'. The pair stood for a while and took in the information. It was clear to

James that they were having a rough day, you could see it in both of their eyes.

'Listen I'm not going to threaten you or do anything bad but I am going to ask you to give me the bag, you're both in way over your heads with this, give me the bag and it will all go away I promise..', James pleaded with the broken pair that stood in front of him, he wasn't willing to play the same game as the violent crooks that ran rampant in search of wealth and reputation. James lit another cigarette as he waited for a response from Eanna and Leah who stood in front of him cold and broken. 'Well unfortunately we don't even have the bag, it was taken off us when we got here', Leah shrugged looking down to the floor.

'We left the station when we got here, we were so careful but these two guys were waiting for us, they had guns and they took the bag from us and told us to leave... now we're on the run and we don't even have the one thing that might have made it worth it'. Leah explained what had happened, Eanna stayed quiet throughout, he was coming to terms with the fact his cousin was dead and that due to the course of events in some ways it was his fault. 'What did these guys look like'? James asked Leah whilst putting on his best detective mind in an attempt to work out the problem.

'I only got a good look at one of them', Leah said, 'he was a lanky guy, around 50, he had slick back hair and a bomber jacket... also he was from Manchester', she continued. James thought long and hard, they weren't the same men from the CCTV footage on the news and it certainly wasn't the original thief, no doubt he was also chasing the bag down as they spoke, or he was very much dead. Something clicked and he made a link, he wasn't sure, but the description sounded familiar, it was the Manchurian accent that stood out, James thought back to the plane. He remembered all the weird interesting characters that had been onboard, the two men making crude jokes and disturbing the passengers. One of them had fitted the description perfectly.

'I think I may have seen these men before', he said out loud whilst thinking to himself. 'there's not a lot I can do to help you guys at this point, but I have a hotel room near the station, you are more than welcome to stay with me there until we all work out our next moves'. Eanna and Leah seemed to gauge each other's reactions for a moment before agreeing, they had nowhere else to go and they both knew they needed to get off the streets, not to mention they were both in desperate need of sleep. James abandoned his hotel room opposite Noah's house, he had used a fake name when he booked in anyway, so it didn't really matter. No one had seen him leave and so it would be easy to just disappear.

The trio walked wearily back towards the central station, they were all overly tired and ready for bed. James thought about getting another cab but figured he didn't fancy any human interaction for now, no one spoke as they trudged back to James's original hotel, they were all too tired and they had all seen too much for small talk. It was easily a half hour walk, James figured that he would ask any questions he had in the morning and then he could get back on the case from there, for now he just wanted to fall asleep to clear his head, no doubt however bad he felt, his friends probably felt worse.

They eventually reached the hotel and crawled lifelessly into the room, James offered Eanna and Leah the bed, they both crashed out almost immediately whilst still almost fully clothed. A small sofa lined one wall and so James found a comfortable angle to pass out in, he didn't remember closing his eyes, all three were too tired to think, they simply shut their eyes and drifted off. They would all worry about their problems in the morning, it wasn't worth thinking about now. No one set an alarm, no one even closed the curtains. The room sat in solitude silence, not a sound, just three lifeless bodies sprawled in their own spaces. The toll of the stress from the day's events could be seen in the frown that was worn on Leah's face as she lay passed out on top of the bed.

From the hotel room if you looked down into the square and beyond the cathedral you could see the tape and distant flashing of the police lights. Detectives were still working hard on the tunnel murder from earlier that evening, Simon's folded body had been removed but police still combed the area for every detail. The police didn't know how yet but they assumed that the two murders that evening must have been related. It was no coincidence that two men had been murdered at the hand of gunmen in one night, it was now down to the detectives to work out why. No doubt the news would be alive with stories of violence and gangster feuds on the streets of Köln the next morning, there was no doubt they would get half of the information wrong.

David and Mike sat in their Audi S8, the engine was off, but they had kept the radio running gently in the background. They sat watching the tunnel murder being cleaned up. 'What do you reckon Mike? It was definitely something to do with the bag, sounds like police are still looking for a positive ID', both men knew that this was no random murder or coincidence. A death like this only happened over an event such as their mission, they knew it was something to do with them, they just hadn't connected the dots yet. 'There's more players in this game than we know about', David comment. They both knew it, what they didn't know was just how many players there were or how they fitted into the puzzle.

'I guess the best thing we can do now is cool off for a few hours and wait to see what information comes out', Mike said, 'I agree, until we know just who or what is going on we're effectively running in the dark.. I still don't think we should have shot that Noah guy… I'm not a big fan of our clients scorched earth policy to be honest mate... the kid would have made good bait and we could have had Eanna and Leah under control by now'. David didn't like how the job was going, things were getting violent, it was all turning into amateur hour and they were stuck in the middle of it. It also didn't help that their employer was very eager to make a point during the operation by encouraging obscene levels of violence at every interval, they had even offered more money to ensure that David and Mike drove the fear of god into anyone that crossed them.

David and Mike debated their next move, the one thing that was clear was that they weren't going to gain much more from staying at the scene. They were better off retreating for the night and picking up any information in the morning, they were hard and good quality operators, but no one could function properly on sleep deprivation. It played strange tricks on the brain, it would slow down motor skills, make simple tasks difficult and sometimes it would make the sufferer begin to hallucinate. The engine of the S8 roared into life, the headlights switched on and the car pulled away and into Köln, they would deal with the mess in the morning.

Chapter 19: A well-deserved holiday

Several weeks had passed and not a whisper had been heard, Lisa sat on a white-hot beach, in one hand she held a bottle of Super Boc beer and in the other she held a joint. She sat up on her elbows and basked in the sun, she did nothing and yet all eyes were on her, she was a beautiful free songbird and passers-by admired her as she pouted to herself. Lisa had run to Lagos in Portugal, it was a small town in the Algarve, it had beautiful white beaches enshrouded by sandy jagged cliffs and caves, the town was a maze of brightly coloured streets and cobbled steps. It was the perfect mixture of tradition, good food and parties. There were loud vibrant bars and clubs dotted around town where young holiday makers threw back shots and took coke before roaming down to the beaches at 2 O'clock in the morning.

Lisa had gone to Lagos for two reasons, the first was it was far away from all the mess in Amsterdam and Köln, the second was that she was in desperate need of a holiday after everything she had been through. She hadn't been on a real holiday in over 3 years, she had already imagined flying away to a beach for a week but Mr Abdi was always scared that if he let his girls go they would never come back, a smile broke out on her face imagining the hideous scars that probably adorned Mr Abdi's face, that prick had deserved everything that came his way, she only hoped he didn't take it out on some other poor girl.

The evening was beginning to close in, and Lisa wanted to hit the town, the parties were always good, and the drinks were cheap. She finished her beer and packed her towel into a rainbow shoulder bag, she threw a long linen shirt on to walk back through the town and a pair of leather strap sandals. She didn't look like an escort anymore, she looked like a beautiful young woman out on an adventure and glowing with life. As she walked through the town, she would stop to look at the shops or to listen to a street musician pouring their soul into the blues whilst sitting on the steps of an old building.

She made it back to the hotel and shook out her hair as she bounced through the front door, the man behind the kiosk smiled and welcomed her back, she smiled back as she wiggled past and into an elevator at the far end of the entrance hall. She kept her pair of cat eye sunglasses on all the way up to her room on the third floor, she walked into her room and turned on a speaker on the bedside cabinet, Witchy woman by the Eagles blurted on. It was a slightly messy room with clothes strewn about the place, she checked under the bed, the black grip was still there. Lisa stripped and climbed into the shower, psychedelic rock rang out through the hotel room and she danced to herself as she cleaned away the sand and salt.

As she stepped back out of the shower, she winked to herself in the steaming mirror, before swaggering back through to the bedroom. She picked out a beautiful red summer dress with a yellow stitched round collar. She spent a moment looking through the various shoes she had bought since arriving and settled on a pair of yellow pumps, it looked beautiful like a summer flower glowing in the morning sun. Lisa didn't wear much makeup anymore, she didn't feel any need to, a thought had also come over her recently to dye her hair a lighter colour, she was thinking a mousy brown with a hint of blonde in the highlights, the new summer vibe suited her.

A line of coke was laid out on the table and she rolled up a note to inhale it, after taking the hit she danced to herself, swaying to the music that filled her room, she was almost ready to hit the town and dance around in the bars. She picked up a yellow clutch bag which hung from behind the door and made sure she had everything she needed for the night out. She then slid open the bedside draw and sat next to the obligatory bible was her handgun, the same Walther PPK that had been used to gun down Simon in the street. She made sure it was loaded and slid it into the bag, she generally didn't go out at night without it, she never knew what might happen or when her decisions might catch up with her.

The best bar in town was Mellow Loco, a small place with a pool table in one corner, tables around the edges of the room and a space in the middle next to the bar that could just about be used for dancing if you wanted to badly enough. The staff were all young people that had visited the town on holiday and simply never left again, a few locals also worked there like the bouncer on the door, and the bar manager, a small guy with ears that poked out at right angles. As was normal in Lagos the spirits were poured by eye and the sizes were often four fingers deep of vodka or rum and a few drops of mixer to help it go down. The dealers didn't even have to hide and simply partied with the rest of the visitors, the police turned a blind eye, it wasn't hard to figure out that they were most likely in on the operation and taking a pretty penny to look the other way.

Lisa stayed for a few hours and danced with strangers, did shots of tequila with the bar staff and took coke in the toilets whilst chatting about the trivial subjects of life and love with new best friends. It was a good night, every night was good in Lagos, she considered never leaving and buying a little flat somewhere so she could live next to the beach and never worry about life again. Everybody who lived there seemed so much more relaxed, she had made a friend whilst she was out there, an English girl named Oli who had come out on holiday and simply never went home, she was blonde with huge breasts and a wild party attitude. Oli could be found cruising the bars and seemed to know everyone, no one was really sure what she did for money but by the amount of coke she took and the amount of drinks she had every night she clearly wasn't doing badly.

Oli and Lisa would talk when they bumped into each other and rate the men in the bar, it was nice to have a cheeky friend like Oli around, it made it easier to be out in a foreign place all alone. Unfortunately, she couldn't find her crazy friend tonight and so Lisa decided it was time to head back to the hotel around 11 before the swarms of party goers began to head to the beaches over the next few hours. She was tipsy and grabbed one last shot for the road, a few Australians at the bar joined her for tequilas, one of them desperately tried to chat her up as she left. Lisa said goodnight to the doorman and went on her way, she lit a cigarette as she walked off into a side road towards the hotel.

The walk back was like every other, the warm breeze blew through her hair and she smoked her cigarette whilst taking in the architecture through the moody streetlights, every so often a piece of graffiti would pop out from a whitewashed wall. She was in no rush and so she enjoyed wondering down the back streets for a little while, that was the beauty of the place, there was never a rush to be anywhere, it was nothing like London that was for sure. Out of nowhere someone grabbed her, Lisa let out a muffled scream through the hand that covered her mouth. A man violently pinned her to the wall and began to touch her, she struggled but he was much stronger.

He groaned something grotesque in her ear in Portuguese that sent a shiver down her spine, she didn't even speak the language, but she had an idea of what he might have been saying. He ran a hand down the inside of her thigh as she tried desperately to break free of his grip. Panic set in and she writhed with all of her energy. Nothing seemed to work, the man spun her around to face him and rammed her to the wall with his thick rough hand around her throat. He tried to lift one her legs to rape her but as he did, she spat in his face. He didn't like that and so he punched her in the stomach, the air evacuated from Lisa's lungs and she gasped for breath as she bent over. The man grabbed her hair and pulled her upright and pinned her back to the wall.

There was nothing she could do to fight it, she couldn't breath and gasped for breath as he ripped away her underwear and slapped her violently across the face before forcing himself inside her. She cried silently, the humiliation and degradation were both worse than the pain. As he had his way with her thrusting like the most disgusting of pigs he forgot about her hand, Lisa slipped her free hand down to her clutch bag and popped it open, inside was the Walther PKK. She forgot about the rape that was taking place as she focused her mind on gripping the handgun in her palm. She could feel the cold steel, she had cocked it before she left and so she flicked off the safety. The pig looked her in the eye and was confused by what he saw, it wasn't fear, it wasn't disgust but controlled vengeful anger. The look on her face drove fear into his heart, by the time he realised it was too late.

Bang! A round ripped through his knee and he dropped to the floor and called out in pain. 'You sick rapist fuck', Lisa screamed at him as she burst into tears. The man held his leg and begged for his life as he tried to slither away into the gutter of the street. Through the tears that ran down her face she aimed the gun at his crotch and fired two more rounds that left a bloody mess where his cock and balls had been. The pig simply cried and writhed in pain, Lisa's yellow pumps trod down in his windpipe so he could scream no more, and his face went bright red before she emptied the rest of the magazine into his bulging hideous face. The gunshots left a speckled red design splattered across her shoes; the holiday had come to an abrupt end.

Sirens could be heard in the next streets over, the police were always ready for trouble in town and so there wasn't long to escape, they would be on the scene in a matter of minutes, she dropped the gun in a panic and ran off down the road. The blue flashing lights reflected off a wall at the end of the road as she turned the corner, she barely made it out of the street before the police cars could be heard screeching to a halt at the bloody crime scene. Lisa felt no guilt, the pig had gotten off light with a quick death, she was only angry that she was now on the run again. It was at that point she realised she had dropped the gun and she cursed herself as she continued to run. She would need to pack and move as soon as she made it back to the hotel, perhaps she had outstayed her welcome in the fun little town of Lagos.

Chapter 20: The evidence doesn't fit

James, Eanna and Leah had joined forces from the hotel in Köln, it was an odd relationship, but they were all determined to come out on top. James had come too far to allow the chase to fall dead at his feet. Leah felt like she couldn't go home, she was stuck as a fugitive until the whole scenario cleared itself up, for Eanna it was personal. He had taken the news of Noah's death badly and felt that if he could get his hands on that bag it would be just a small victory over the people who had gunned down his cousin, he would make them pay for what they had done one way or another.

The hotel had become a hive of activity over the last few weeks the walls were covered in newspaper articles from the original robbery up until the most recent murders of Noah and Simon, they had pictures of the two military men that had chased them through Amsterdam and a mugshot of Simon from an article all on a wall. They had tried to make sense of the sequence of events and compared each other's stories to understand where they all fitted in the puzzle. Most of the information was fairly straight forward and they were all unsure what to actually do with it but there was one thing that stood out to James in particular.

James had remembered the other man who had been with Colin, it would seem that someone had been betrayed in that tunnel, considering both men went in to ambush Eanna and Leah yet only one of them had walked back out, but something didn't add up with that narrative. The footage from the murder showed the second man running out of the tunnel except he didn't have the bag in his hand when he left. Why would he have shot his partner and then left without the one thing they had been fighting over in the first place? It simply didn't make sense. The other thing that stood out was reports of a red VW Polo that had been spotted both before and after the events, it was allegedly driven by a woman who police were hoping to question, the car had been running on fake number plates and there had been no sign of it since.

James had a hunch that something didn't add up in the tunnel and that the red polo was far more important than anyone had realised. He had an idea but beyond that he had no way of acting on it, without being able to trace the number plate or access to CCTV from the night there was nothing he could do about it. He was back to praying for a miracle and the chances were he was fresh out of those. He had already stumbled over enough luck in the past month since the whole ordeal had started. The room was smoggy with the combined of all three smoking constantly, they scoured the internet for information, articles and newspaper cuttings scattered the walls and floor of the hotel room. Sitting on one side was a bottle of cheap whisky and a bag of weed Leah had gone out to acquire a few days before.

They decided to take a break and sat together on the double bed, they had all become quite close over the last few weeks whilst locked away in the tight little hotel room. They had a common aim and a desire to see the whole thing through to the end even if deep down James was giving up hope. Leah flicked on the tv at the end of the bed and lit a joint whilst leaning back into the pillows. She flicked through the channels and settled briefly on the news, another murder by the looks of things, this time it was in Portugal. The footage showed a police officer being interviewed with several microphones shoved in his face.

None of them understood a word the officer was saying but they did understand one thing, he uttered the words Walther PKK. Something clicked and all three of them looked over to the same article on the wall in unison, an article with a picture of Simon and next to it a picture of what the police believed had been used to shoot him, written in bold letters underneath the firearm was the words Walther PKK. They all stared at it for a moment unsure if it could really be that easy, Eanna rolled off the bed and pulled the article from the wall and began to scan through it before finding a passage to read out loud to the room.

'Police believe that the murder weapon involved in the shooting was a Walther PKK, they are requesting anyone with information to come forward and are looking for a man and a woman who were both seen fleeing the scene separately'. He read out in his thick Irish accent. 'Well it's got to be fucking one of them', he deducted, the trio looked to each other with a sense of excitement, they were back on the trail, if they could get down to Lagos then maybe just maybe they would be able to get their hands on the bag after all. They went to work immediately collecting any information they could about the most recent murder, James took notes from what he could work out from the news channel whilst Eanna and Leah scoured the internet together on a beat-up old laptop. Before long they had pulled up an article saying a young woman had been seen fleeing the scene.

They began to pack their few belongings away, they collected any evidence of their investigation and shoved it all into a rucksack. There was little they would be able to do about the state of the room and so they hoped that they could check out before anyone was able to see the state it had been left in. It stank of cigarettes and weed, and weeks' worth of takeaway boxes and empty beer bottles stacked up around the bin and on surfaces. Being a detective was a messy business apparently, it didn't help having three people crammed into a small room for a long period of time. All things considered they had put up with each other pretty well.

They finished packing the bags and left quickly, he had been paying in cash so there was no way they could track him down once they were gone. It was the best way to operate considering the circumstances, the ragtag crew exploded out of the hotel and into the street, it was the first time any of them had experienced proper sunlight for several days and so they squinted as they shifted down the road like drunks awakening from a perpetual hangover. It was decided that the trains would be too long and too risky considering that Eanna and Leah were still on the run and so it was agreed that the best thing they could do was rent a car and taking the roads instead.

There was a car rental company at Köln airport naturally, James worked out the details whilst his convict friends waited outside. It wasn't pretty but he could get a Skoda Scala for around £38 a day, it would be perfect for the job and blended into the traffic well. The deposit was astronomical, the whole trip had ripped through his savings, he needed to get the bag soon just to keep up with the lifestyle he was buying into. The woman at the counter handed over the keys after showing him the navy-blue car, they loaded the boot with the bags, all three jumped in and they were away on the road to Lagos.

Chapter 21: Hunting Lisa

David and Mike sat outside in the warm breeze, the local fish in Lagos was exquisite and fresh out of the sea. They had dressed down into shorts and short sleeved shirts with rucksacks that contained any equipment they might need. They both wore bum bags that no one was aware held their Walther P99's and a spare magazine, to any passers-by they were simply tourists enjoying a meal, their sinister intentions were well hidden in the happy little town. They had traced the red VW polo out of Germany towards Portugal several weeks before and last night's murder had confirmed their suspicions that they were on the right trail. A single phone call had provided the men with the information they needed to take the next steps; they were on the hunt for a former escort.

It was the woman from Charlie's office in Soho, he had heard that one of Charlie's girls had left him in quite a mess, it must have been her, Mike almost admired the balls on the girl to take on Charles Abdi, run away to Amsterdam and then commit several murders and get away with a grip bag worth millions. It would almost be a shame to kill someone so beautiful and so feisty he thought. The murder of the local man had left the pair scratching their heads, there was no way he could have been caught up in the whole affair, the best they could think of was either a rape or robbery gone wrong, if so they had no sympathy for the fat corpse.

Dave pulled a brown envelope from his bag that had been printed and delivered that morning, he flicked through it, it was a police file, a picture of Lisa sat inside. Lisa was known for prostitution and had been charged with assault when she punched a police officer during a raid a year or so ago in London, other than that her record was clean, she was originally from Lithuania. 'She won't be hard to find I reckon', he commented as he passed the file across the table to Mike who had a flick through for himself. If Lisa was in town there was no doubt, she would have found her way onto the party scene, the professionals decided that their best point of call would be the network of local drug dealers who supplied the clubs.

David paid the bill at the restaurant and they both left, an email came through on his phone as they walked out, it was a list, a list of local coke and weed dealers in the town. The plan was simple, turn up at a few doors and ask some questions, if the person on the other end didn't want to play the game all they had to do was remind them how easy it was to ruin someone's day with a simple phone call and a few local cops on the payroll. The first on the list was Miguel Silva, a 32-year-old man who had previous for supplying drugs to tourists. The local police had been instructed to take someone down in order to make it look like they were taking care of business and Miguel had been getting too sloppy with his work and had even been heard bragging about being untouchable. It was all part of the game at the end of the day.

He lived in a small house in one of the many back streets that spiralled around town, a dog barked incessantly as the Audi pulled up outside. The men stepped out of the car in unison and closed the heavy doors behind them. An old woman watched them with a scowl as she hung up washing from a balcony. Mike banged on the door loudly and sharply three times. Inside a woman could be heard calling out and a brief argument took place before with little warning the door opened ajar with a small crack and a man's face poked out. 'Are you Miguel Silva'? David asked with a blank expression. 'Yes', Miguel said, he didn't dare close the door, he had seen men like them before.

'Miguel we are looking for this woman, we think she's in Lagos and there's a good chance she's hanging out in the party scene, we know what you do for business and figured you might have seen her around', David showed Miguel a picture of Lisa as he explained the situation. The man looked down at the photograph for a short while and contemplated before looking back to David. 'I'll be honest man, I don't deal in the clubs anymore, I have runners for that, I can keep an eye out but right now I know nothing', Miguel explained. He was upfront and honest with the two men, he knew better than to cause himself problems, it was bad for business.

David thanked him, 'keep the photograph', he said, he also handed Miguel a piece of paper with a number to contact him on. 'If you manage to find the girl, let us know, our client will pay good money for information leading to her', with that the two men left and stepped back into the Audi that was parked directly outside. 'Well that's one down, who's next on the list'? Mike asked as he turned the key and the engine came to life. 'Next, we have Alfonso Nevasca, a 24-year-old coke dealer who operates out of the bars, he's pretty low in the chain but he has a lot of face time with the customers. David figured that if anyone had seen Lisa around town, he was the best bet.

It wouldn't have taken long to get to the house if it wasn't for the narrow old streets that caused horrendous traffic on the best of days. If they didn't have all of their equipment sitting in the boot, they probably would have parked the car up and simply walked it instead. What should have been a ten-minute drive dragged on to become an endless stream of traffic jams and impatient twiddling of thumbs and drumming on the steering wheel. Eventually they made it to the address and managed to park not too far away, it was a flat on the third floor, this would prove to be a little trickier as they would need to persuade him to buzz them in.

Mike pressed the buzzer and they waited patiently for a response, what sounded like an elderly woman answered the buzzer and spoke to them in Portuguese, they had no idea what she was saying and so simply said the young man's name to gauge a response. 'Alfonso'? Mike asked in a polite voice, the woman continued to talk to them in Portuguese and so Mike tried to communicate with her again, 'Alfonso Nevasca'? He asked again, 'We would like to speak with him, is he here'? There was silence at the other end. The line went dead, and the two men were left outside to decide how to approach the problem.

After waiting for a few minutes hoping that someone might return to the block in order to allow them through the first door a sheepish young man appeared in the doorway, he had mid length curly hair and wore shorts and a t-shirt with flipflops. From behind the door he assessed the men that had come to see him, he seemed nervous, he wouldn't be wrong to be. 'Alfonso'? Mike asked again, 'yes that is me, what do you want'? the young man asked. 'We are looking for someone and we were hoping you might be able to help us', Mike explained whilst trying to appear none threatening. 'Who are you looking for'? the young man asked, he seemed slightly confused by the predicament. David produced the picture of Lisa and held it up to the door 'we want to find this woman; do you know her'? he asked. 'I have seen her around... yes', the young man nodded as he said it.

'Where did you see her'? Mike asked, 'well I've seen her hanging around in the bars sometimes, she has been here a little while... I think she goes to Mellow Loco a lot... is she in trouble'? Alfonso couldn't work out the men that stood in front of him, they carried themselves like police officers, but they were English, and they were dressed like tourists. He didn't dare ask who they were or what they wanted, and he certainly wasn't going to open the door for them. 'Thank you', Mike said and they both walked off without another word, they didn't need any more information from the young dealer, they knew she was in town and they knew where she was likely to hang out. From there it would be easy to pin her down.

That afternoon the red VW Polo was found parked down a side street, the police found it before David and Mike which wasn't great, it was lifted from the street and taken for forensics, the pieces of the puzzle were slotting together and the links had been made between the tunnel murder and the murder of the fat man. It would only be a matter of time until some detective worked out the connection back to the London robbery. It had also come to the two professional's attention that the police in Amsterdam had now found the burnt-out car with Elliot Wicks inside. That was of little concern for them as there was no DNA trace to lead back to the two men. The trail of blood and bodies would eventually lead like breadcrumbs to the bag.

The important thing was that the professionals knew that Lisa was still in town, if she had any sense at all she would be packing her bags at that very moment and preparing to leave. She had left enough evidence to close the net down on herself and it was only a matter of time. The clock was ticking and David and Mike now needed to find the woman before the police did otherwise the bag could be lost to the authorities and the next time anyone would see it would be as evidence in an international murder case, they couldn't let that happen.

Chapter 22: The raid

Lisa felt scared, she had left her hotel room first thing in the morning after the man had attacked her, she didn't know what to do, she was used to that sort of abuse but this had been different, she was meant to be safe now and it had come out of nowhere. No doubt the police would be looking for her and so in her panic she took a single suitcase and the black grip bag. She decided to abandon the car, she was sure someone would have found it by now. She walked across town in the early morning sun with her hood up and her head down, she was hoping no one would recognise her, the paranoia ate away at her as she walked through the streets.

She booked into a new hotel using a fake name and paying in cash, the whole time she felt watched. It was as if at any moment the walls were going to cave in and she was going to be rushed by gangsters or police officers, she even thought about handing herself in and finishing the whole ordeal once and for all. The concierge smiled politely to her and booked her into the room, 'you will be in room 39', she said and guided Lisa towards the elevator with her hand. Lisa was quick to get away from the prying eyes of the public and so she thanked the woman behind the counter and walked briskly towards the elevator and pressed the button.

It took a few minutes to come, those few minutes felt uncomfortable and long, she gripped her bags tight and tried to hold herself together in the man reception without causing a scene or drawing attention. All Lisa really wanted to do was burst into tears, but she held it back, she was stronger than that. Eventually the lift came, and she stepped inside, it climbed to the third floor and she took a left into the corridor of identical doors until she reached room number 39. When she arrived something seemed off, the door was already open, and the lights were all turned off inside. Perhaps the cleaners had forgotten to close the door she thought, she stepped into the dark room and put down her bags before turning around to close the door and turn a light on.

Lisa turned back around and gasped, it was the man from the tunnel. 'Sit down', Colin said calmly whilst sat back in a chair, he was holding his pistol ready to fire which leant on the knee of his leg that was crossed across his body. He held his signature wicked smile as he watched her slowly take a seat on the corner of the bed, she was truly helpless and had no way out. She placed her hands on her lap and simply stared down to the floor, unwilling to make eye contact with her fate. She only had one question for the man with the gun, 'how did you find me'?

Colin was more than happy to answer, in fact he was quite proud of his handy work, it had taken a certain amount of skill and cunning to catch Lisa out and also he was wired on cocaine and so he was more than happy to tell a short story. 'Well you see my love... when you shot Simon... thanks for that by the way, as I ran away I managed to spot your car as I ran out of the tunnel, I knew it was yours because the plates were from Amsterdam which seemed too much of a coincidence.. so I managed to remember the number plate and tracked it, I tracked it by working out which motorway you had taken out of the city and from there it was simply a matter of working out where the car appeared. Once you arrived in Lagos I simply followed you for a while, I have been breathing down you neck for almost a week and you didn't even know... as for getting into this hotel room, I was literally stood behind you and whilst you waited for the lift I made a mad dash up the stairs to beat you and used a master key to break the lock.. and here we are'.

Colins monologue rambled on until he was satisfied with gloating over his ingenious plan to find her. It had taken hours of scouring stolen and hacked motorway footage, but he had managed it and all by simply calling in some favours from a few hackers in the squat scene back in London with a heroin problem and some serious debts. A tear rolled down Lisa's face at the realisation that it was over, and she had lost, perhaps there were to be no winners in the dangerous little game that she had played. Still she said nothing, she had lost the bag and there was nothing she could do, if she was lucky, she might still escape with her life. It was a that moment the blue light began to bounce off the walls from outside in the street.

The lights caught both of their attentions and Colin stood up to briefly look out of the window, the police had arrived in force and were beginning to storm the building, there was only one reason they could be there, the net had closed in on Lisa. Colin kept the gun trained on her as he walked towards the door and picked up the black grip bag on his way out. 'Farewell and good luck', he said with a wink once he stepped outside and slipped the pistol away under his jacket. Colin walked calmly down the narrow hallway and to the stairs, he always preferred the stairs, you could always make an escape on the stairs. He jubilantly bounced down into the reception area where the first officers were storming through and up the staircase he had just come from, as he walked out of the building he smiled and waved at them like a stupid tourist.

Multiple cars had skidded to a halt and parked at precarious angles outside the front of the hotel on the main road. The lights flashed and flickered, making blue shapes jump out on every surface, Colin simply had to walk between them and to freedom, no one suspected a thing. He grinned like a Cheshire cat as he strolled down the sun soaked street, in some ways the silly little girl had done him a favour by blowing Simons brains out, it had taken the attention away from him and it had also taken out a major problem he didn't even known he had. She may have also tried to kill him but ironically, she had saved his life. Whatever was actually in the bag would be going back to London with him and funding whatever venture he deemed fit for his next adventure, he promised himself that he wouldn't invest the profits too wisely, that would be no fun otherwise.

Chapter 23: Stakeout

James sat at the wheel of the unexciting navy-blue Skoda, Eanna and Leah sat in the back. All three had cigarettes on the go and waited at the side of the road on the main street in Lagos near the beach. It would have been easy to forget why they were there and just walk onto the beach, as they smoked, they all worked their way through burgers, the car was a mess and well lived in. 'So now what'? Eanna asked through a mouthful of food. 'I'm not quite sure', James responded whilst looking in the rear-view mirror. 'I guess we find a hotel and set up our base of operations, maybe see if we can find that car or wait for something drastic to happen', James was barely able to finish his sentence when a convoy of police cars rolled past where they were parked.

It must have been at least 8 cars and a few vans all with blue lights flashing and moving at speed. Instinct kicked in and James pulled out of the parking spot to the surprise of the pair in the back who were thrown back as he pulled away, Leah dropped her burger in the process. He accelerated to stay with the racing formation but stayed far enough back to not alert their attention. The lights changed up ahead, he ran the red to the crescendo of car horns as he sped through. 'What the fuck are we doing'? Leah shouted from the back, 'I have a hunch that wherever that convoy is going could lead us exactly to where we want to be... it's worth a go I guess', Eanna and Leah clung on for dear life in the back as James tried desperately to keep up with the convoy ahead.

With little warning the cars all came to a sudden halt outside a large hotel on the main strip, officers poured out of the cars and into the lobby whilst others began to do crowd control outside. 'This has to be it', James whispered to himself as he pulled into a new parking spot on the near side of the road. 'I think we found them', James said looking back at his partners with a grin on his face. Whoever was responsible for the murder of Simon and the man in Lagos had to be inside, he figured that they probably weren't the only people descending on the scene either. All they could do for now was sit in the car and wait and hope the police weren't going to beat them to the prize.

David and Mike sat on the opposite side of the road directly in front of the hotel, they knew Lisa was inside and had been waiting for the right moment to act, the police arriving had changed their plan massively though. They waited to see what would happen, if she tried to escape then they could pick her up and finish the job and disappear with no issues. It had also come to their attention that the other man from the tunnel murder was in town and had been asking questions, his name was Colin Lear and had a criminal record as long as his arm, the professionals remembered him from Suzie's bar. They had put an insurance policy in place just in case Colin fucked everything up too much, but that would be a worst-case scenario.

It had been several minutes since the police had swarmed the scene and there was no sign of Lisa being dragged out in handcuffs, there was also no sign of the bag which in reality was probably a good thing, if they couldn't get the bag back then the orders were to destroy it and blowing up government property normally ended in tears. As the men sat waiting intensely a lanky figure appeared walking out of the hotel and cutting his way through the police officers who were charging in. It was Colin and he had the bag; he had a stupid grin on his face and waved at the officers as he skipped off down the road and away from the scene.

It was far too risky to take any action and so David and Mike stepped out of the car, pulled a bag from the boot and began to follow him. It was the height of the day and people and police were everywhere, the officers all armed and ready to go. They would have to play the situation very delicately; it would be best to follow Colin for a while and see where he was going. They walked up the hill behind him which looped around and back into town, they would tail him for a while and pick the right moment to get the bag and leave. They were armed and dangerous, around this town the car would be useless so they kept it parked at the hotel, any dirty work would need to be done on foot.

James, Eanna and Leah watched the raid taking place from just up the hill, 'Oh fuck!' Eanna burst out, he dived for cover and grabbed Leah to get down as he did it. It was Colin, he passed them by with a swagger in his step, it looked as if he thought he had won. 'that was him! That was the man from the tunnel', Leah said, 'and it looks like he has the bag', James added as he looked at black grip in the mirror once Colin had passed him by. 'Well ladies and gentlemen this is it, let's get that bag', they waited for a minute until Colin was almost out of sight before getting out of the car and following him on foot. James was really starting to wish that he had a gun right now, he had a feeling that it could all get very ugly.

Lisa bowled out of the rear fire exit of the hotel and into an alley way, she had abandoned her room and sprinted out of the hotel in panicked determination whilst the police had stormed the building in search of the female cold blooded killer. She looked around from left to right and made her way through the back streets in search of Colin and the bag, Lisa wasn't prepared to give up on her freedom that easily. In her hand she held a piece of brick she had picked up off the floor, she was expecting the worst to happen. As she turned a corner a young officer stood in front of her completely taken by surprise. Before he could draw his Glock or his baton, she had charged him down and struck in in between the eyes with the chunk of brick. He tumbled backwards onto the floor and she hit him a few more times for good measure, Lisa took his gun and continued on her journey.

Chapter 24: The great crescendo

Colin had made it up the hill and followed the road around back into the old town blissfully unaware of the host of characters who were following him to his demise. He hummed a tune to himself as he proudly skipped down the tight streets and high walls that were bleached white, the smell of the fresh sea and the salt wafted through the air, it was the smell of freedom and a job well done. The wall exploded next to him as he met some crossroads and he spun on his feet as a gunshot rang out, the shot had been dangerously close but as people should have been aware by then, Colin didn't die that easily. As he turned around, he made eye contact with David and Mike for the first time. They had slowly been closing the gap on their victim from the opposite side of the road. Mike dived behind the wheel of a parked car as Colin drew his gun and let off several rounds that peppered the far wall.

David fired back rapidly as Colin slithered around the corner and out of sight, David had dropped the kit bag, opened it and pulled out one of the MP5K's and slid the bag over to Mike who was stepping back to his feet. They ran off after Colin whilst covering their arcs as they did so. The chase was on, it had begun. James, Eanna and Leah had crumpled into a small alley way with some bins and now picked themselves back up to re-join the chase, shots rang out and they followed the sounds of violence at speed. People screamed and ran the other way or dived for cover. They sped past a poor old woman who had been clipped in the crossfire, it sounded like she was praying, and she held a cross that had been around her neck. What no one saw was Lisa stood down another alley with a smoking barrel and cursing herself at missing Colins head.

Lisa took a different route to the others but also followed the sounds of gunshots ringing out down the alleys. The whole thing spilled out into one of the main streets filled with restaurants and tourist shops. Lisa slid behind a pillar of a restaurant and began firing wildly which caught Dave totally off guard who then turned and fired a burst of 9mm in her direction before changing his firing position. Colin sat behind a wheelie bin with the bag and rolled out to take a shot at Mike who returned fire that peppered the metal bin with holes that punched straight through to the other side. Colin realised the cover served no purpose and moved his position to a corner made up of brick work.

James, Eanna and Leah had managed to burst out of a side alley and straight into the crossfire of the gun fight. They tumbled and slid across the road as objects around them exploded in a hail of fire. They found themselves ducking in the doorway of a sushi restaurant. A waitress decided to make a mad dash for freedom and erupted in a red mist and collapsed as the violent rounds ripped through her body, she was dead instantly, another man further down the street had caught a round in his femoral artery and clung to his leg in terror as he bled out onto the cobbled steps. There were only brief pauses as parties stopped to reload.

Eanna had seen enough and began to throw beer bottles in angry protest at the violence that ensued, he may not have had a real weapon but Noah would be avenged and so the beer bottle warrior took his brave stand huddled in the doorway of the cheap tacky restaurant. Leah peered inside the open door and her eyes lit up, she became transfixed on the katana that sat on the wall above the bar. She slipped inside to grab it, as she did so a burst of rounds ripped through the restaurant, it was amazing that Leah wasn't hit, she didn't even notice, she was drawn towards the sword like a moth to a lamp. James looked around and tried to work out how to get close to the bag, perhaps if they went through the restaurant and out flanked Colin who stood at the furthest end of the fight.

David and Mike took turns firing whilst the other broke cover to close in on their victim, Lisa still sat behind her pillar and wildly let rounds off from the stolen police Glock. It was at this point the first officers arrived on the scene, the volume of fire increased massively as the various criminal parties stopped focusing on each other a drew their attention to the police who had skidded around the corner with weapons drawn. The first skidded around the corner and immediately his eyes widened at the scene in front of him, he was riddled with rounds and dropped to the floor almost immediately leaving speckles of bright blood like a Jackson Pollock painting on the white wall behind him. With his last breaths he gasped and coughed blood whilst watching the chaos unfold in front of him.

Another officer dropped next to the sushi restaurant and James took the chance to grab the pistol out of his hands and join the fire fight. Every so often a beer bottle or bottle of spirits would launch from Eanna's position that would then smash and leave the gunmen ducking or covering their eyes. Leah sat wild eyed clutching her katana, she had always wanted one and she was just caught up in the moment.

Colin took the distraction of the police arriving to make a dash for it, he ran off from the scene, James let off his first round in Colin's direction as he fled and then grabbed his friends to make a mad dash through the bullets once more in pursuit of the wealth. Once more rounds embedded themselves in walls and exploded around them as they sprinted. An officer sprung up in front of them, they bumped into each other as they came to a screeching immediate stop. He held a gun in Leah's face who with no hesitation let out a Kungfu movie style yelp before relieving him of his hands. They still clutched the gun as they dropped to the floor, the scene became a blood orgy fitting the most outrageous of Japanese samurai flicks.

Everyone looked at her in stunned shock, even the officer, who then screamed as he looked at his handless arms squirting fresh blood out into the road. They had no time to think about what they had just seen and so everyone kept running after Colin. The fact that the gunfight didn't get any further away suggested that the rest of the players were also in hot pursuit. In the wake of the gunfight lay dead and wounded officers and civilians who had been caught in the crossfire, it looked like a savage and violent war had taken place. For a short while the shooting stopped, and shouting could be heard. The streets were alive with the sounds of running down towards the sea and the docks.

Colin was the first to burst out of the old town and onto the sea front, he was almost home free, a police car stopped violently in front of him. It was driven by a single policeman who was hit in the arm by one of Colins rounds as he ran along with the bag in hand. He launched over the bonnet of the car and continued to run down towards the sea front and towards the docks, he was almost runover by the oncoming traffic in the process. The next to appear was Lisa who had collected another handgun on her travels and now fired wildly with fresh ammunition. None of the rounds landed home but bounced off the road and pavement around the thin man as he gasped for breath on the home stretch.

The two professionals were nowhere to be seen and the automatic fire could no longer be heard ringing out in the streets, the final party to appear were James, Eanna and Leah. They sprinted straight past Lisa with little thought and followed Colin in hot pursuit who had now made it to the docks that were lined with fishing boats and small white yachts. Lisa joined the three in hot pursuit, no longer concerned with the others that surrounded her. As the party made it to the dock Colin threw himself into a speed boat that sat at the end and quickly untied it. More rounds sprayed splinters up into the air as Lisa and James both tried to end their target.

Colin managed to get the boat untied and revved the engine into life before speeding off into the waves whilst cackling to himself in his wicked laugh. James, Eanna, Leah and Lisa all made it to the end of the dock and gasped for breath, Lisa emptied her final magazine in Colins direction and screamed dramatically as she did it. Rounds splashed around the boat and after a few seconds the only sound coming from her gun was a clicking and the slide sat back to show that it was empty. All four stood in disbelief, they had all come so close in their own ways and now they witnessed the bag float away on a boat into the distance.

Boom! A fireball rolled into the sky and they could feel the heat on their faces, the boat exploded without warning and seemingly without reason. Shrapnel and pieces of debris flew into the air, James could have sworn he witnessed an arm fly into the distance through the carnage. All four characters stood with their mouths open and totally unsure how to react to the situation. As the fireball receded all that remained was flames and bits of wreckage floating on the water and bobbing in rhythm with the waves.

David and Mike stood back on the beach front with a smile on their faces, they both held their weapons in their hands and David held a mobile in the other. He had rung a number from the phonebook saved under the name fireworks. The fireworks hadn't disappointed, it was time to go home. David slipped the phone back into his pocket and watched the fireball for a second. James looked back from the dock at the professionals, they did nothing but simply nodded and smiled in his direction, the game was over for them there was no more need for any violence. The two professionals dropped their weapons and walked off casually back in the direction of their car; it was just after they fell out of sight around a bend that the sirens began to sound once again.

James, Eanna, Leah and Lisa all stood quietly at the end of the dock as the sounds of sirens grew ever louder. Over head the sound of a helicopter could be heard and behind them doors slammed shut and weapons were drawn and cocked ready to fire. To this day they weren't sure who started it but someone began to laugh quietly under their breath. Before long, it became infectious as each of the characters slowly began to burst into laughter, none of them exchanged a glance or a final moment, they simply looked out to sea and the burning fire in front of them and laughed. Behind them a swarm of police officers sat ready to apprehend the crooks who had instigated one of the most violent criminal acts in the region's history. James tossed his handgun into the sea with minimal effort, put his hands in his pockets and walked back towards solid land with a gentle smile upon his face.

Lightning Source UK Ltd.
Milton Keynes UK
UKHW012217030321
379729UK00001B/69

9 781839 754722